ALSO BY ANNE TYLER

If Morning Ever Comes (1964)
The Tin Can Tree (1965)
A Slipping-Down Life (1970)
The Clock Winder (1972)
Celestial Navigation (1974)
Searching for Caleb (1976)

THESE ARE BORZOI BOOKS,
PUBLISHED IN NEW YORK
BY ALFRED A. KNOPF.

Earthly Possessions

EARTHLY POSSESSIONS

Anne Tyler

Alfred A. Knopf   New York   1977

THIS IS A BORZOI BOOK
PUBLISHED BY ALFRED A. KNOPF, INC.

Copyright © 1977 by Anne Tyler Modarressi

All rights reserved under International and Pan-American Copyright
Conventions. Published in the United States by Alfred A. Knopf, Inc.,
New York, and simultaneously in Canada by Random House of Canada
Limited, Toronto. Distributed by Random House, Inc., New York.

Library of Congress Cataloging in Publication Data
Tyler, Anne.   Earthly possessions.
I. Title.
PZ4.T979Ear   [PS3570.Y45]   813'.5'4   76–41222
ISBN 0–394–41147–1

Manufactured in the United States of America

Earthly Possessions

1

The marriage wasn't going well and I decided to leave my husband. I went to the bank to get cash for the trip. This was on a Wednesday, a rainy afternoon in March. The streets were nearly empty and the bank had just a few customers, none of them familiar to me.

Time was when I knew everybody in Clarion, but then they opened the lipstick factory and strangers started moving in. I was glad. I have lived in this town all my life, thirty-five years, forever. I liked having new people around. I liked standing in that bank feeling anonymous, with some business-suited stranger ahead of me in line and someone behind me wearing a slithery-sounding, city-type nylon jacket. I didn't know the teller either. Though she might have been one of the Benedict girls, just grown up a little. She had that Benedict voice that turned off and on in the middle of words. "How would you like that, sir?" she asked the man ahead of me.

"Fives and ones," he said.

She counted out the fives, then reached into some inconvenient place and came up with a couple of stacks of ones in brown paper bellybands. Just at that moment, the nylon jacket started up behind me. Somebody pushed me, somebody stumbled. There was this sudden flurry all around. A nylon sleeve swooped over my shoulder. A hand fastened on the stacks of bills. I was extremely irritated. Now look, I wanted to say, don't be so grabby; I was here before you were. But then the teller gave a squawk and the man ahead of me spun in my direction, unbuttoning his suit coat. One of those plumpish men, puffy-faced as if continually, just barely, holding in his anger. He fumbled at his chest and pulled out something stubby. He pointed it at the nylon jacket. Which was black— the sleeve, at any rate. The sleeve darted back (the hand clutching money) and circled my neck. For a moment I was almost flattered. I curved to make way for the object pressing into my ribs. I smelled the foggy smell of new dollars.

"Anybody move and I'll kill her," said the nylon jacket.

It was me he meant.

We backed out, with his sneakers squeaking on the marble floor. Like a camera zooming away I saw first a few people and then more and more, all their faces very still and turned on me. My view grew even wider, took in the whole gloomy, paneled interior of the Maryland Safety Savings Bank. We lurched backward out the door.

"Run," he told me.

He gripped my sleeve and we ran together, down slick wet sidewalks. We passed a man with a dog, one of the Elliott children, a woman pushing a stroller. You'd think they would look up, but they didn't. I considered stopping very suddenly, asking someone strong for help. (The woman with the stroller is who I'd have chosen.) But how could I visit this affliction on them? I was in quarantine, Typhoid Mary. I didn't stop.

In fact for a while there I imagined I might outdistance him, but his hold on me was very tight and he stayed beside me. His feet slapped the pavement steadily, unhurried. While I myself was gasping for air, my handbag thumping against my hipbone, loafers squelching water, and by the third block it seemed that some sharp-edged mainspring had snapped loose inside my chest. I slowed down.

"Keep going," he said.

"I can't."

We were in front of Forman's Grocery, comfortable Forman's Grocery with its tissue-wrapped pears. I stopped and turned to him. It was a shock. I had been building this picture of him in my mind, somebody evil-faced, but he was just ordinary, calm-looking, with a tousle of oily black hair and black-rimmed, pale gray eyes. His eyes were level with mine; he was short, for a man. No taller than I was. And much younger. I took heart.

"Well," I said, panting, "this is where I get off, I guess."

Something clicked on his gun.

We ran on.

Down Edmonds Street, past old Mr. Linthicum, who'd been placed on his stoop as always, rain or shine, by his daughter-in-law. But Mr. Linthicum only smiled, and had long ago stopped talking anyway, so there was no hope there. Down Trapp Street, past my aunt's brown duplex with the wooden eyelet lace dripping from all the eaves. Only she would be inside now, watching "Days of Our Lives." A sharp left down an alley I hadn't known existed, then left again, dodging under somebody's stilt-legged porch, where once, I believe, I played as a child, with a girl called Sis or Sissy, but I hadn't thought of her in years. Then across the gravel road by the lumberyard—does it have a name?—and up another alley. In the alleys it was raining, though elsewhere the rain had stopped. We were traveling a corridor of private weather. I had lost all feeling and seemed to be running motionless, the way you do in dreams.

Then, "Here," he said.

We were facing the rear of a low, dingy building, buckling clapboard in a sea of weeds and potato chip cartons. Not a place I liked the looks of. "Head around front," he told me.

"But—"

"Do like I say."

I tripped over a mustard jar big enough to pickle a baby in.

Then think how I felt when we reached the front and I saw that it was Libby's Grill—only Libby's. Which was also the local pinball joint and bus depot. It's true that I wasn't exactly known there (I couldn't afford to eat out, didn't play pinball, never traveled), but at least it was public, and there was a good chance someone inside might recognize me. I walked in the door as straight as possible. I looked all around the room. But there was just a stranger drinking coffee at the counter, and the waitress was nobody I'd seen before.

"When's the bus leave?" the bank robber asked her.

"What bus?"

"Next one."

She looked at a wristwatch that was safety-pinned to her bosom. "Five minutes back," she said. "He's late as ever."

"Well, me and her want two tickets to the end of the line."

"Round trip?"

"One way."

She went over to a drawer, pulled out two ribbons of tickets, and started whacking at them with a set of rubber stamps that stood beside the percolator. Now, surely people didn't come in every day asking for tickets to the end of the line, wherever it was, on the next bus going out. And surely she didn't often see a woman draggly-haired, out of breath, about to collapse from running too hard, accompanied by a stranger all in black. (For even his jeans were black, I saw now, even his sneakers—everything but his startling, white, out-of-place shirt.) Wouldn't you think she would give us at least a glance? But no, she kept her eyes down, her chin tucked into her other chins, even when accepting the money he laid on the pads of her palm. Before we were halfway out the door, I believe, she had forgotten we existed.

And then the bus had to wheeze up the moment we arrived at the curb, not giving me two seconds to look around for someone familiar. Though I was calmer now. It didn't seem so likely he would shoot me with people around—even these numb, dumb people lining the bus, half of them asleep with their mouths open, old lady talking to herself, soldier with a transistor radio pressed to the side of his head. Dolly Parton was singing "My Life Is Like Unto a Bargain Store." The vanity case on the old lady's lap was meowing. I decided there was hope. I sank into a seat and felt suddenly light-hearted, as if I were expecting something. As if I were going on a *trip,* really. Then the bank robber sat down beside me. "You keep on behaving and you're going to be fine," he whispered. (He was a little out of breath himself, I saw.) He reached over, palm down. His hand was square and dark. What did he want? I shrank away, but he just took hold of my purse. "I'll be needing that," he said.

I disentangled the strap from my shoulder and gave it to him. He held it loosely, between his knees. I looked away. Outside my window was Libby's Grill, the bus driver joking with the waitress on the stoop, a child mailing a letter. What about my children, would they wonder where I was?

"I have to get off," I told the bank robber.

He blinked.

"I've got children, I didn't make arrangements yet for after school. I have to get off."

"What you expect *me* to do?" he said. "Look, lady, if it was up to me we'd be twenty miles apart by now. You think I planned this? How was I to know some clown would pull a gun?" He swung his eyes around, checking out the sleeping faces. "Nowadays just anybody's got them, people without a lick of sense. I could be clean free and you safe home with your kids by now if it wasn't for him. Guy like that ought to be locked up."

"But we're out. You've escaped," I told him.

I felt embarrassed; it seemed tactless to discuss the situation so openly. But he didn't take offense.

"Wait and see," was all he said.

"Wait for what?"

"See if they can say who I was. If they can't I won't need you. I'll let you go. Right?"

He gave me a sudden smile he didn't mean—short, even teeth, surprisingly white. Stubby black lashes veiling whatever look was in his eyes. I didn't smile back.

The driver climbed on, a man so heavy that we felt the tilt when he landed. He pulled the door shut and ground the motor. Libby's Grill slipped away like something underwater. The child at the mailbox vanished. Then the laundromat, the hardware, the vacant lot, and finally the pharmacy with its mechanical lady lounging in the window, raising her arm to rub Coppertone on it and dropping it and raising it again, eternally laughing her faded laugh inside her dusty glass box.

2

I was born right here in Clarion; I grew up in that big brown turreted house next to Percy's Texaco. My mother was a fat lady who used to teach first grade. Her maiden name was Lacey Debney.

Notice that I mention her fatness first. You couldn't overlook fatness like my mother's. It defined her, it radiated out from her, it filled any room she walked into. She was a mushroom-shaped woman with wispy blond hair you could see through, a pink face, and no neck; just a jaw sloping wider and wider till it turned into shoulders. All year round she wore sleeveless flowered shifts—a mistake. Her feet were the smallest I have ever seen on a grownup, and she owned a gigantic collection of tiny, elegant shoes.

When she was in her mid-thirties—still a maiden lady teaching school, living in her dead father's house beside the

Texaco station—a traveling photographer named Murray Ames came to take her students' pictures. A stooped, bald, meek-looking man with a mustache like a soft black mouse. What did he see in her? Did he like her little feet, her fancy shoes? At any rate, they married. He moved into her dead father's house and turned the library into a portrait studio—an L-shaped room with an outside entrance and a bay window facing the street. You can still see his huge old complicated camera there on its stand beside the fireplace. Also his painted backdrop—blue, blue sky and one broken-off Ionic column—which so many schoolchildren used to stand in front of so long ago.

She had to quit teaching; he didn't want a wife who worked. (He was given to fits of cold, black moodiness that scared her to death, that made her flutter all around him wondering what she'd done wrong.) She sat home and ate chocolate caramels and made things—pincushions, Kleenex-box covers, Modess-pad lady-dolls to stand on bureau tops. This went on for years. Every year she got fatter and fatter, and had more trouble moving around. She tilted at each step, holding herself carefully like a very full jug of water. She grew listless, developed indigestion, felt short of breath, and started going through the Change. She was certain she had a tumor but would not see a doctor; only took Carter's Little Liver Pills, her remedy for everything.

One night she woke up with abdominal spasms and became convinced that the tumor (which she seemed to picture as a sort of overripe grapefruit) had split open and was trying to pass. All around her the bed was hot and wet. She woke her husband, who stumbled into his trousers and drove her to the hospital. Half an hour later, she gave birth to a six-pound baby girl.

I know all this because my mother told me, a thousand times. I was her only audience. In some way, she'd grown separate from the rest of the town—had no friends whatsoever. She lived her life alone behind her gauzy curtains. Yet I believe that once my mother's family was very social, and filled that house with dances and dinner parties. (My grandfather was involved in politics somehow, something to do with the governor.) There are pictures of my mother in a pink tulle evening gown, looking like a giant hollyhock, playing hostess in the period after my grandmother's death. In all the pictures she is smiling, and has her hands linked across her stomach as if hugging herself for joy.

But my grandfather was the only man who ever totally approved of her (he called her his biscuit, he loved her dimples, he was glad she wasn't all skin and bones, he said) and once he had died, her social life began to thin out. Pretty soon only her father's oldest, kindest friends asked her places, only to dull family dinners where there was no need to pair people; and then they died, too, and her one lone brother was married to a woman who didn't like her; and the other teachers were so young and vivacious, they filled her with despair. Also, she got the feeling sometimes that the children at school were laughing at her. While they were her pupils they just loved her, oh, they loved to be rocked by her when they fell off the jungle gym and to smell the velvet rose fastened to her bosom, with its drop of L'Heure Bleu she put on a single petal every morning. But a year or two later, when they had passed on to other grades— well, several times she had noticed things. Little snickers, traded glances, rude limericks she wouldn't lower herself to repeat.

Then after she was married there was a brief flurry of invitations, as if she had suddenly been declared alive after a long misunderstanding. But . . . what was the trouble, exactly? She couldn't say. Couldn't put her finger on it. Her husband just never had learned to fit in, maybe that was it. He wasn't outgoing enough. He acted so glum, wouldn't raise his eyes when spoken to and hardly spoke at all himself. Hung about as if he didn't own his body—shoulders sagging, middle caved in; he looked like an empty suit of clothes. No wonder their life had shrunk and dwindled so!

Yes, I wanted to say, but what about Alberta, the lady next door? *Her* husband was no good whatsoever, and still she had more friends than I could count.

I entered school, a whole new world. I hadn't had any idea that people could be so light-hearted. I stood on the edge of the playground watching how the girls would gather in clumps, how they giggled over nothing at all and told colorful stories of family life: visits to circuses, fights with brothers. They didn't like me. They said I smelled. I knew they were right because now when I walked into my house I could smell the smell too: stale, dark, ancient air, in which nothing had moved for a very long time. I began to see how strange my mother was. I noticed that her dresses were like enormous flowered undershirts. I wondered why she didn't go out more; then once, from a distance, I watched her slow progress toward the corner grocery and I wished she wouldn't go out at all.

I wondered why my father had so few customers, most of them soldiers or other transients, and why he had to talk to them in that mumbling, hangdog way that tore at my heart. I worried that he and my mother didn't love each other and would separate, fly apart, forgetting me in the flurry. Why couldn't they be like Ardle Leigh's parents? The Leighs held hands every place they went, but my parents never touched at all. I seldom saw them look at each other. They seemed to be staring inward, like people cheated or disappointed somehow. And though they slept in the same great wooden bed, the middle of it stayed perfectly neat—a median strip unrumpled, undisturbed. Or sometimes they quarreled (irritable lashings-out, no issue you could *name*, exactly) and my father spent the night in his studio. Then I felt dislocated and sick to my stomach. I loved my father more than I loved my mother. My father believed I was really their true daughter. My mother didn't.

My mother believed there'd been a mix-up at the hospital. It was all such a shock, that whole business, she said; she'd been a little dazed. An unexpected birth is like—why, an earthquake! a tornado! Other natural disasters. Your mind hasn't quite prepared a frame for it yet. "Besides," she would say, plucking at the front of her dress, "they gave me some kind of laughing gas, I think. Then everything was a dream. My vision was affected and when they showed me the baby I assumed it was a roll of absorbent cotton. Mostly they kept her in the nursery. On the day I went home they handed me this bundle: a stark-naked child in a washed-out blanket. Why! I thought. *This* is not mine! But I was still so surprised, you see, and besides didn't want to make trouble. I took what they gave me."

Then she would study my face, with her forehead all ridged and sorrowful. I knew what she was wondering: what stranger's looks had I inherited? I was thin and drab, with straight brown hair. Nobody else in the family had brown hair. There were peculiarities about me that no one could explain: my extremely high arches, which refused to be crammed into many styles of shoes; my yellowish skin; and my height. I was always tall for my age. Now where did that come from? Not from my father. Not from my mother's side—my five-foot mother and her squat brother Gerard and her portly, baby-faced father beaming out of the photo frames, and certainly not from my Great-Aunt Charlotte, for whom I was named, whose pictures show her feet dangling comically when she is seated in an armchair. Something had gone wrong somewhere.

"But of course I love you anyway," my mother said.

I knew she did. Love is not what we are talking about, here.

Unfortunately I was born in 1941, when Camp Aaron was filling up with soldiers and Clarion County Hospital suddenly had more patients—mainly soldiers' wives, giving birth —than at any other time before or since. All the hospital's records for that period are skimpy, inaccurate, or just plain lost. I know, because my mother checked. She had nothing to go on. Somewhere out in the world her little blond daughter was growing up with a false name, a false identity, a set of false, larcenous parents. But my mother just had to live with that, she said. Her hands fluttered out, abandoning hope.

To her the world was large and foreign. I knew that it was small. Sooner or later her true daughter would be found. Then what?

My father, if asked directly, said that *I* was the true daughter. He didn't go on and on about it; he just said, "Of course." Once he took me into a guest room and showed me my baby clothes, packed away in a brassbound trunk. (I don't know what he thought that proved.) He had had to buy those clothes himself, he said, while my mother was lying in the hospital. He had bought those clothes for *me*. He jabbed a finger at my chest, then scratched his head a moment as if trying to recall something and went off to the studio. I worried that he was building toward one of his moods. I barely glanced at the baby clothes (yellowed, wrinkled, packed together so long and so tightly you would have to peel them away like cigar leaves) before I left too and went to find him. I worked alongside him all afternoon, rinsing heavy glass negatives under running water, but he didn't say anything more to me.

Meals were strained and silent: only the clinking of silverware. My parents didn't speak, or if they did, it was in a hopeless, bitter way. "Bitter as acorns," my father said, and he set the coffeecup down so sharply that it splashed across the mended tablecloth. Then my mother lowered her face to her hands, and my father jerked his chair back and went to wind the clock. I mashed my peas with my spoon. There was no point in eating. Anything you ate in that house would sit on your stomach forever, like a stone.

These were my two main worries when I was a child: one was that I was not their true daughter, and would be sent away. The other was that I *was* their true daughter and would never, ever manage to escape to the outside world.

3

I was glad the robber had let me have the window seat. Even if it wasn't out of the kindness of his heart, at least I got to see the last of Clarion skating by. Followed by a string of housing developments, and then wide open fields where I could just sit back and let my eyes get lost. It was years since I had been anywhere.

Meanwhile there was this nylon jacket slicking around to one side of me, continually changing position. He was restless, I could tell. I mean restless in a permanent way, by nature. At all stop signs and traffic lights he resettled himself. When a woman rose to get off by a mailbox in the middle of nowhere I heard his fingers drumming, drumming, all the time the bus was stopped. Once we had to slow down behind a tractor and he actually groaned out loud. Then shifted his feet, scrunched his shoulders around, scratched his knee. With his left hand, of course. His right hand was out of sight—arm folded across his stomach, gun jammed between my third and fourth ribs. He was taking no chances.

What did he think I would do? Jump out that little, sooty window? Ask the old lady in front of me for help? Scream? Well, scream, maybe; that might work. (If they didn't just think I was a lunatic and pretend not to hear.) But I am not the kind to scream, I never have been. As a child I nearly drowned once, sinking in a panic beneath the lifeguard's eyes with my lips clamped tightly together. I would rather die than make any sort of disturbance.

We rode alongside a freight train a ways. I counted the cars. If you're stuck you're stuck, I figure; might as well relax. I wondered why the B & O Railroad had changed its name to the Chessie System. Chessie could be a new kind of sandwich spread, or a lady gym instructor.

From time to time it occurred to me that I could possibly be killed in a while.

The soldier's radio was playing a golden oldie, "Little Things Mean a Lot." I could close my eyes and be dancing at the Sophomore Prom again if I wanted. Which I didn't. The song broke off in the middle of a high note and a man said, "We interrupt this program to bring you a special bulletin."

The bank robber didn't move a muscle, but he grew a surface of awareness that I could feel.

"Clarion police report that the Maryland Safety Savings Bank was robbed at around two thirty this afternoon. A white man in his early twenties, apparently working alone, escaped with two hundred dollars in one-dollar bills and a female hostage as yet unidentified. Fortunately, the bank's automatic cameras were activated and police have every hope of—"

The soldier turned a dial on his radio. The announcer lost interest and wandered away. Olivia Newton-John drifted in.

"Shoot," said the robber.

I jumped.

"What's a two-bit place like that want with cameras?"

I risked a glance at him. There was a little muscle flickering near the corner of his mouth. "But listen—" I said. The pistol nudged me, like a thumb. "Listen," I whispered. "You're gone now! You're out of there."

"Sure. With my face all over a roll of film."

"What does that matter?"

"They'll identify me," he said.

Identify? Did that mean he was a known criminal? Or paranoid, maybe—some maniac from Lovill State Hospital. Either way, it didn't look good.

"It don't look good," he told me.

His voice was thin and gravelly—the voice of a man who doesn't care what he sounds like. I wasn't encouraged by it. I shut my mind and turned back to the window, where peaceful farms were rolling by.

"What are you staring at?" he asked.

"Cows," I said.

"They're going to meet me at the next town, wait and see. What's the next town?"

"Now listen," I said. "Didn't you hear the radio? They know you have a hostage, that's all they know yet. They're looking for a man who's traveling with a hostage. All you've got to do is let me go. Doesn't that make sense? Next place we stop at, let me off. You stay on the bus. I won't say a word, I promise. What do I care if they catch you or not?"

He didn't seem to have heard. He gazed straight ahead of him with that muscle still working. "One thing I cannot abide is being locked up," he said finally.

"Right."

"Can't take it."

"Right."

"You're staying with me till I see that bank film."

"What?"

"Half the time them things're all blurry anyhow," he said. "Why panic? We'll wait and see. If the film's no good, if they lose my tracks, why, then I let you go."

"Well—how will you *know* the film is no good?"

"They show it on the tube," he said. "Evening news, I bet you anything."

"But where will you get to watch it?"

"Baltimore, where'd you think."

He let his head fall back against the seat. I returned to looking at farms. I thought I had never seen anything so heartless as the calm, indifferent way those cows were grazing.

We must have been on the most local kind of bus it is possible to get, because we stopped at towns I'd never heard of before and a lot of other places besides. Crossroads, trailer parks, lean-tos covered with election posters. By the time we reached Baltimore it was twilight. I could look out the window and see my own reflection gazing back at me, more interesting-looking than in real life. Beyond was the outline of the bank robber, constantly shifting and fidgeting.

At the terminal, our headlights colored a wallful of black men in crocheted caps and satin coats, lounging around chewing toothpicks. "Balmer!" the driver said, and the passengers rose and collected their things. All but me and the bank robber; he held me down. He made me wait till the others were past. Now it was *my* turn to get fidgety. I have a little trouble with closed-in spaces. If a bus isn't running its motor it is definitely a closed-in space. "I need to get off," I told him.

"You'll get off when I say so."

"But I can't stand it here."

His eyes flicked over at me.

"Do you want me to have hysterics?"

I wouldn't really have had hysterics, but he didn't know

that. He stood up and motioned me into the aisle with a gleam of his pistol. We followed the soldier, whose radio was playing "Washington Square." For some reason I always get "Washington Square" mixed up with "Midnight in Moscow" and it wasn't till I was all the way off the bus, standing in a daze on the concrete and teetering from the long ride, that I decided it was "Washington Square."

"Will you move it?" the robber said.

Couples were meeting and kissing in the gray light between buses. We dodged them and headed toward the street. There were a lot of people milling around there, mostly men, mostly no-account. It was the hour for getting off work but that wasn't what they were doing here, surely—standing about in packs, loitering in front of cocktail lounges and peep shows and "Girls! Nitely!" There was a strong smell of French fries. Everybody looked dangerous. But I had this robber and his warm heavy gun, and anyway, what was left to lose? He was the one with the purse. I slid through the crowds as easily as a fish, unhampered, guided by that nudge in the small of my back.

"Stop," he said.

We had come to a dingy little place with a neon sign sizzling in the window: BENJAMIN'S. A red wooden door so thickly painted I could have scratched my name on it with a fingernail. He pulled it open and we went inside. A TV set turned the air blue and dusty; rows of bottles topped with silver globes glittered before a mirror. We felt our way to the bar and sat down. I unbuttoned my raincoat. A man in an apron turned his cheek to us, while his eyes stayed fixed on the television.

"What'll you have?" the robber asked me.

At our house, nobody drinks; but I didn't want to seem unfriendly. "Pabst Blue Ribbon," I said at random.

"One Pabst, one Jack Daniel's neat," said the robber.

The bartender poured Jack Daniel's blindly, while watching a commercial for potato chips. But he had to turn away to hunt a glass for my beer. Then the news began and he gave up, passed me a stark tall can unopened and held out his palm for whatever money the robber put into it.

Various politicians were traveling around the countryside. We saw them getting off airplanes, setting right in to shake hand after hand like people hauling rope. We saw a man who'd been acquitted by a jury. He believed in the American system of justice, he said. There was a commercial for Alka-Seltzer.

"Hit me again," the robber told the bartender, holding out his glass. I opened and took a sip of my beer. The good thing about sitting at a counter was that I didn't have to look at him. We could each pretend the other wasn't there.

My eyes were used to the dark by now and I could see that this place was hardly better than a barn—barren, dirty, cold. It would have been cold even in July; no sunlight ever reached it, surely. I wondered what the restrooms were like. I needed to go to one but I wasn't certain of the procedure.

They had never covered *this* problem on those cops-and-robbers shows.

In the local news, there was a school board meeting. A policeman's funeral. A drug arrest. A five-car accident in Pearl Bay. A bank robbery in Clarion.

The announcer's face gave way to film of a different quality, blurred and shadowy. On this film a small group of people stumbled in line, like dominoes. The foremost person, a squat man in a business suit, tore something from his chest. An arm loomed out. Another man backed jerkily away, half hidden by a tall, thin woman in a light-colored raincoat. The man and woman disappeared. Several faces swam forward, and someone put a white scarf or handkerchief to his or her eyes. I was fascinated. I'd never before been able to observe a room after I had left it.

The announcer returned, a little blank of face as if he'd

been caught unawares. "So," he said, and cleared his throat. "Well, that was . . . and remember you saw it here first, folks, a genuine bank robbery in progress. Police have identified the suspect as Jake Simms, Jr., a recent escapee from the Clarion County Jail, but so far no one has stepped forward to name his hostage. However, roadblocks have been set up and Clarion's police chief Andrews feels confident that the suspect is still in the area."

"Come on," said Jake Simms.

We slid off our stools and left. In the doorway I glanced back at the bartender, but his eyes were still on the screen.

"I knew it would work out like this," the robber told me.

"But you're *past* all the roadblocks."

"They're looking for me by name."

We threaded our way through even larger crowds than before, none of them apparently going anywhere at all. As far as I could tell, the gun wasn't jammed in my back any more. Was I free? I stood still.

"Keep moving," he told me.

"I want to find the bus station."

"What for?"

"I'm leaving."

"No, you're not."

We stood square in the middle of the sidewalk, blocking the flow of pedestrians. He needed a shave, I saw. It made me uneasy to be at eye level with him; I distrust compactly built men. I reached out a hand, careful to make no sudden moves. "Could I have my purse, please?" I said.

"Look," he told me. "It ain't *me* keeping you, it's them. If they would quit hounding me then we could go our separate ways, and believe me, lady, there ain't nothing I'd like better. But now they have my name, see, and will track me down, and I need you for protection till I get to safety. Understand?"

We went to another bar, as dark as the first but with some

customers in it. This time we sat at a little wooden table in the corner. "Now let me think. Just let me think," he told me, although I hadn't said a word. Then he gave his order to the waitress: "One Jack Daniel's neat, one Pabst. Couple bags of pretzels." I decided not to drink the Pabst because of the restroom problem. I folded my arms on the table and craned my neck to see the TV—this one in color, a man reeling off the weather. Meanwhile, Jake Simms set my purse on the table between us. "What you got in here?" he asked me.

"Pardon?"

"Any weapons?"

"Any—no!"

He undid the catch and opened it. He pulled out my billfold, frayed and curling. Inside was a pathetic bit of paper money. Small change and bobbypins. A library card. He glanced at it. "Charlotte Emory," he said. He studied a photo of me holding Selinda, back when she was a baby. Then he looked into my face. I knew what he was thinking: lately I had let myself go. However, he didn't comment on it.

He pulled out a rubber-banded stack of grocery coupons, which made him snort; a pack of tissues, an unclean hairbrush, and a pair of nail scissors. He tested the point of the scissors with his thumb and then looked at me. I was still focused on the hairbrush; it had disgraced me. I didn't connect. "No weapons, huh," he said.

"What?"

The waitress brought our order and presented him with the bill. While he was rummaging in his pocket I sent her silent messages: Doesn't this look odd to you, this man emptying out a lady's purse? Don't we make a strange couple? Shouldn't you be mentioning this to someone? The waitress merely stood there, gazing dreamily into the marbled mirror above us and holding out her little plastic change tray.

When she had left, Jake Simms dropped the scissors under

the table and gave them a kick. I heard them scuttle across the floor. Then he reached into my purse again. This time it was a paperback—my *Survival Book*, worn to shreds. How to get along in the desert. He frowned. Turned the purse upside down, shook it—and out clattered something shiny which he trapped immediately. "What's this?" he said, holding it up.

Oh, Lord, my badge. Little tin badge, shield-shaped, like something official or military. "I'll take that," I told him.

He looked suspicious.

"Can I have it, please?"

"What is it?"

"Well, it's just a—like a lucky piece or something. Can I have it?"

He squinted at the writing across its face. "Keep on *truckin'?*" he said.

"I believe it's from a cereal box."

"Kind of trashy, for a lucky piece."

"Well, it's just from a box of . . . something or other, what does it matter?" I asked him. "*Most* lucky pieces are trashy. Rabbits' feet, two-headed pennies . . . I found it in a cereal box while I was eating lunch today. I think it's some kind of popular saying. I was going to throw it out except—oh, *you* know how your mind works. I took it as a sign. Not seriously, of course. I just thought, what if this was trying to tell me something? Like to get on the road, not sit around any longer, take some action."

"Now, how'd you come to *that* meaning?" he said.

"I thought it was a sign to leave my husband," I said.

There was a silence.

I asked, "Could I have my badge back?"

"Let me get this straight," he said. "You were leaving your husband."

"Well, *you* know . . ."

I held out my hand for the badge. He ignored it. "I'll be damned," he said. "Things've finally started going my way."

"What?"

"And here I was cursing my luck! Thinking I had put myself in some bind here! Waiting for your people to set the FBI on me! Oh, your fortune's changing, Jake, old man."

"Well, I don't see how—how—"

"Things are looking up, it seems to me."

"I want my badge back," I said.

"Nope. Think I'll keep it. Medals have pins, pins are deadly weapons."

"It's not a *medal!* It's a little old, dull-pointed, cereal-box . . ."

But he dropped it in his shirt pocket, and I had to watch it go.

Then suddenly I got scared. I don't know why. I mean I don't know why *then,* just at that particular moment. But all at once I felt short of breath and shaky, and it didn't seem to me that I had any way out of this. Nothing had prepared me! I was so peaceful, hated loud noises, passed sharp objects handle first. And I didn't like confronting people face to face, even, let alone fist to fist. I took a tight hold on the table. I tried to get my air back. I fixed my eyes very hard upon the TV, which was no help at all: bandits on thundering horses. Old-fashioned train wheels clacketing past, a man leaping from saddle to baggage car in a slow high arc that was nearly miraculous. Some of the people at the bar started cheering.

"Yeah, well," said Jake Simms, "that's the trouble with these things. You watch long enough, you start expecting some adventures of your own."

I let out my breath and stared at him. From this close I could see the graininess of his skin, the smudges under his eyes, and his thin, chapped, homely-looking mouth. But he was concentrating on the TV still, and he didn't notice me.

By the time we got outside again it was really night. I rebuttoned my coat. He turned up his collar. We trudged down a

corridor of neon signs and music, took a right turn onto a
darker street. Now we passed pawnshops, luncheonettes, cleaning establishments. We saw a laundromat where solitary people
were folding up their bedsheets.

In the window of an appliance store, six TV sets showed a
woman shampooing her hair. Then a news announcer mouthed
something grave. Then Jake and I came on the screen and
backed away: our same old soundless, hobbled dance. We
stood at the window watching ourselves through the outline of
our reflections. We were locked together forever. There was no
escape.

4

This wasn't the first time I'd been kidnapped. It had happened once before.

Here's how it came about: I was entered in a Beautiful Child Contest at the Clarion County Fair. I was entered because the first step was to send in the child's photo. If I won, it would be good advertising for my father. In fact I remember the large white letters that ran across the bottom of my picture: PHOTO BY AMES STUDIOS. Ordinarily, he just rubber-stamped that on the back.

In this picture my hair was wetted down, hanging in neat straight clumps to my jawbone. My expression was meant to be fierce but came out sad. (Nothing they could do would make me smile.) I wore a dark jumper over a puff-sleeved blouse. My mother thought puffed sleeves would make me look younger. I was seven at the time, the top age permitted in the contest. There was a lot of talk about how I'd been much rounder-faced and—well, cuter, really, when I was six. My mother wished with all her heart that there'd been such a contest when I was six.

But even so, a letter came saying I'd been chosen for the finals. I had to show up at ten a.m. on the opening day of the fair, they said. Right before the Miss Clarion Contest. After the Beautiful Babies.

My mother made me a dress of white eyelet. Although she hadn't been anyplace in years, she said she was coming with me to the fair. She told me this while she was pinning up my hem. I went rigid. How would she manage such a thing? She sweated and puffed even crossing a room; she traveled in a casing of thick, blind differentness. And lately she'd started breaking whatever she sat upon. Horrible things had happened at our house that would have been very embarrassing if witnessed by an outsider. She would have to take her special chair along— her heavy white slatted one with the stolid legs, the kind you ordinarily see in people's yards. She would not be able to climb any wooden steps or stand on any platforms. "Let me out!" I cried.

Her arms fell to her sides. Since I was standing on the dining room table at the time, she had to tilt back to gape at me. "What's wrong?" she asked.

"Let me out! Let me out! Let me out of this!" And I began tearing at the billow of white eyelet.

"Charlotte? Char, darling? Sweetheart!" she said, batting my hands down. "Charlotte, what's happened to you?"

Then my father came in, shuffling along in his corduroy bedroom slippers. He was sunk in one of his moods. You could tell by his face, which seemed to have stopped trying. He turned his droopy eyes in my direction. "I have to get out of this!" I told him.

"Lord yes, you look like a chimpanzee in a ball gown," he said.

He went on through to the kitchen.

My mother slowly, gently helped me free of my dress, while I stood still as a statue. She folded it and laid it on the table. She stroked the ruffle that edged one puffed sleeve. I knew what she was thinking: if only it were her *true* daughter entering this contest!

Both of us wished it could have been.

We rode to the fair with our only relatives—my fat Uncle Gerard, his wife Aster who didn't like us, and Clarence, their son, a huge lumbering marshmallow ten years old. Uncle Gerard drove us in his Cadillac, which felt so close and tightly sealed I wasn't sure we'd have enough air for the trip. We didn't take Mama's chair because for that we would have needed the pickup. She was just going to stay on her feet the whole time. And I had to sit next to Clarence, who breathed through his mouth. He had adenoid trouble. I looked hard out the window, pretending I was somewhere else.

It was 1948 and the countryside, now that I think back on it, was as peaceful and well-ordered as an illustration from a Dick-and-Jane book. Lone gasoline pumps, fields flowered over like bedspreads. Trees turning perfectly red and perfectly yellow. At the entrance to the fairgrounds, a billboard showed a lipsticked, finger-waved housewife holding up a jar of home-made preserves. CLARION COUNTY FAIR, OCT. 9–16, the billboard said. A TIME FOR PRIDE. My uncle slowed down at the ticket booth and held a fistful of dollars out the window. "Four adults, one child," he told the attendant. "We won't need a ticket for this other child. She's here by invitation, going to be in a beauty pageant. My niece."

He believed every word he read; he really did think it was a time for pride.

The contest was held in the Farm Products Building, amongst the eggplants and butter pats. I don't remember the contest itself but I do remember the building, with its cavernous, echoing roof and bare steel rafters. The little girl next to me had speckled legs because of the cold; she worried that the judges would think she was *always* speckled. There was a smell of roses. No, the roses came later. They were set in my arms when I won. My picture was taken by a man who was not my father.

I know that picture line for line, by now; it used to hang in the upstairs hall. An 8 x 10 glossy showing a blur of children in white or light-colored organdy, eyelet, and dotted swiss; and front center (stiller than the others, and therefore clearer) a dark little girl in a dark plain school dress, carrying roses. Actually, she doesn't seem all that beautiful. I believe the secret of my success was the orphanish clothing, the straight hair that my mother had given up on, and my expression of despair. The Little Match Girl. How could they bear to hurt my feelings?

The winner of the Baby Contest was packed in her carriage and sent on home, never to be heard from again. Miss Clarion appeared on stage every night before the rodeo. But the Beautiful Child was not so lucky. I had to stay in the Farm Products Building. Every day from three to six (after-school hours) for a solid week I had to take my place on the splintery gold-painted chair in the center of the platform. I wore a paper crown and held a scepter, actually a hot-dog skewer covered with flaky glitter. I can see it all still; I remember everything. The pumpkins on the pumpkin table below me, each on its separate paper plate. The hatted, aproned farm wives casting sideways glances at the jams, where prizes had already been awarded. The children carrying balloons with "Hess Fine Fertilizer" swelling across them. And the dark-haired woman who stood in front of me hour after hour, day after day, staring up into my face without a hint of a smile.

She was pretty in a stark, high-cheekboned way that wasn't yet fashionable. Her coat was long and narrow, and I had never seen legs so slender. I liked her two feverish spots of rouge but I wasn't so sure of her eyes, which had a sooty appearance. You couldn't help wondering what had gone wrong, looking into eyes like that.

People swirled past her like water around a rock. She ignored them. She stood with her hands jammed deep in her pockets and gazed only at me.

Meanwhile, ladies came up to tell me how cute I was. Children made faces at me. Cousin Clarence (my only chaperone, now that the contest was over) washed in on a tide of old men from the nursing home and washed out again, splayfooted. The woman and I continued to stare at each other.

On the afternoon of my last day at the fair, when it was almost time for my parents to arrive, the woman stepped forward and raised her arms. I rose and laid aside my scepter. I removed my crown and set it on the throne. Came down the stairs to meet her. She took my hand. We left by the end door.

We cut across the midway, passing various booths where you could win a teddy bear by ringing bottles, piercing balloons, or throwing nickels into slippery china plates. So far I'd seen only the educational exhibits and I was hoping the woman would stop here, but she didn't. Nor did she offer me a ride on the Ferris wheel. One glance at her face told me it was out of the question; she had something serious on her mind. She walked quickly, frowning a little. I took a tighter hold on her hand and scurried to keep pace.

We went on to where the fields took over and a wind blew up to make me shiver in my short-sleeved dress. The sun had set by now. Against the flat gray sky I could make out a group of trailers. They must have been there all week; the ground around them was churned and hardened. Some flew strings of flapping shirts, some had motorcycles beside them, some were lit with soft yellow lights. The trailer the woman took me to was dark. It had no clotheslines or other appurtenances anchoring it down. The woman flung back the door and reached inside to switch on a lamp. I stood looking into what might have been a doctor's waiting room—bare and neat, upholstered in shades of tan.

"Go in, please," the woman said.

I stepped inside. The woman closed the door behind us and walked to the dark end of the trailer, still wearing her coat, briskly rubbing her fingers together. "It's so cold!" she said. "I will make us some tea." I could tell she had a foreign accent but I didn't know what kind. We didn't have any foreigners in Clarion. "Do you drink tea now?" she said.

"No," I said.

Instead of offering anything else, she stopped rubbing her fingers and came back to the living room. She sank onto the edge of the daybed and I sat down beside her. She turned and searched my face. "Do you like it here?" she asked.

"Yes," I said.

"It means nothing to me," she said.

I could see that it wouldn't.

"Anyway, everything is his. I require a bureau drawer, only a bureau drawer. I keep even my shoes in the drawer, even my coat, my dress. So, if I am a little wrinkled you will understand why."

I took a quick look at her coat. It didn't seem wrinkled. To me, she was perfect. She had set her feet together so neatly they looked like empty shoes beside a bed. Her hair was darker than mine, but I recognized it by the way it hung.

"He himself has *three* drawers, and a closet," she said. "He has offered me another drawer but I tell him I don't need it."

I nodded. I thought she was right.

"But do you believe this of me? When you remember how much I *used* to have? My life has changed. He says, 'You must get another dress, my God, you're not a refugee any more.' 'I don't have room for another dress,' I tell him. I let him buy me only things that won't take space—meals in restaurants and trips to beautiful scenery. I love to travel. Oh, don't you love to travel?"

I blinked.

"You think I'm mad," she said.

What would she be mad about?

"You suppose I would be tired of travel forevermore."

"I think traveling would be fun," I said.

"Fun," she echoed.

We stared at our laps a while.

"You were the first," she said finally. "After that, the baby fell ill, I don't know with what. Then Anna said, 'I won't go on.' 'You must, it's such a short way now,' I told her. In truth, I had no idea how far it was. We had been walking for days, weeks, I don't know. Perhaps months. The bottoms of our feet were bloody. We were eating grasses. When we heard a noise and hid I wasn't frightened any more. What did it matter? But Anna was frightened. One day I looked around and she was gone. Maybe she had been gone a long time. I had nothing left. I had only my dress. Then I started traveling for its own sake and would put first this foot, then that foot. Then this foot, then that foot. I must tell you that I didn't think of you at all any more."

"That's all right," I said.

"I was so, you see, so interested in putting one foot and another. I would say to myself, 'I have nothing.' I liked that. I enjoyed it. Did you know all this?"

I shook my head.

She turned, so suddenly she startled me, and took my face in both her hands and drew me close. I hadn't realized how shaky she was. "Say it," she said. "Do you forgive me?"

I said, "Sure."

Her hands dropped and she sank back.

Then she said, "Well!" She was smiling. She sat up, tossed back her hair. "We must find something for you to do," she said. "It's boring for you, no? We will see if he has anything interesting."

She began stalking around the trailer, assembling objects. "Scissors. Paper," she said. She spread them on the coffee table. "Colors. No, he would never have colors."

Still, she looked for some, opening and slamming doors at the dark end of the trailer. "No. No. We will have to use pencils," she said. "This man is poorly supplied." She returned with two stubby pencils, one of which she handed to me. "We are making paper dolls," she told me. "You love making paper dolls."

"Yes," I said. I didn't question how she knew.

I cut dolls in strips, the way I'd been taught in kindergarten—rows of children in triangular dresses, holding hands. But the woman made hers one by one, and each was different. First a man, then a girl, then an old lady with skinny ankles. She drew in their features with a pencil. She gave them the simplest clothing—just a line here and there to show a sleeve or a hem. As each was finished she set it down to join the others on the coffee table, all those white paper legs striding in the same direction. It seemed we were seeing people off, somehow. But I didn't know what it meant.

Then the door burst open and a big blond man stepped in, wearing a black leather jacket. "That goddam Bobby Joe," he said. "What time is it? I told him, I said, 'Bobby Joe . . .'"

He stopped. He looked at me. The woman went on with her work. He said, "Now, what in . . . ?"

The only sound was the cool metal chewing of the scissors.

"Oh, Jesus," he said. He dragged his hand across his face; he might have been wiping off spiderwebs. "You're that little girl," he said.

"Huh?"

"Aren't you? You're that little girl that everyone's been looking for."

He turned back to the woman. "Jesus," he told her.

She went on snipping. In the curve of her lids I read the truth: she wasn't going to save me. She felt herself to be somehow in the wrong. She was like certain children who grow deaf and closed in and stubbornly silent when a grownup scolds them. It was up to me.

"I live here," I told the man.

He grunted, gazing out the dark window as if there were something there that mattered more.

"I do! I live here! She's my true mother. I'm her true daughter."

"Did you have a coat?" he asked me.

I glanced down at myself. "No."

"Jesus. Come on."

If the woman had said one word, or held out a hand or given me a single look, I would have fought him. But she was concentrating on the curls of a paper child. When the man took my arm, I went quietly.

We made our way through a deeper darkness than I had expected, toward a blur of red and blue lights. Now the midway had a whole new crowd of people and louder music, but the man rushed me so that I barely had time to see. We went to an office in a Quonset hut. (I had thought we were headed toward Farm Products.) In a tiny cold room that smelled of cigars, my parents sat before a desk where a man was talking on the telephone. My father leapt up as soon as he saw me. My mother's mouth fell open and she held out her hands. Tears were streaming down her face. I went to kiss her, but my mind was on her chair—a wooden desk chair. Would it hold her? Would it break, would she find herself stuck between its great curved arms when she rose to go? Now, when I think back on that reunion, the only thing I remember clearly is that breathless moment when my mother shifted her weight, rocking on those four matchstick legs, and collected herself and rose—oh, working free after all!—to totter over to my father and ask him for his handkerchief.

I rode home in the pickup, on the slippery seat between my mother and father. My mother kept stroking my hair, talking on and on, sometimes losing her thread. "You see first we thought you were just . . . oh, and they hardly bothered, I mean ordinary people don't care really, do they? 'Now, getting excited never helped a thing,' was all they'd say. 'Excited?' I said. 'She's been *kidnapped!* You tell me not to get excited?'"

But I wasn't listening, at least not with both ears. I was letting a thought start to form in my mind. A plan. A picture of my future. How was I to know this picture would stay with me forever after, never go away, haunt me even when I was grown and married and supposedly sensible, occupy all nights I couldn't sleep and all empty moments every day of my life?

In this picture, I am walking down a dusty road that I have been walking for months. The sky is deep gray, almost black. The air is greenish. From time to time a warm and watery wind blows up. I am carrying nothing, not even a bite to eat or a change of clothes. The soles of my feet hurt and I am stringy-haired, worn down to bone and muscle. There is no house or landmark in sight, no sign of life. Though sometimes I have an impression of other, anonymous people traveling in the same direction.

Since October 16, 1948, I have been trying to get rid of all belongings that would weigh me down on a long foot-march. I loved, in 1948, a woolly gray doll, once blue, with a plastic face—a Sleepy Doll, it was called, because its eyes were eternally shut, two painted crescents of lashes—and I planned to take it with me, but as I grew older I gave up on that idea. Later I was going to take my charm bracelet, with its tiny silver hourglass containing real sand, but the bracelet got lost during a school trip to Washington. In a way, I was relieved. It would only have been a burden.

My life has been a history of casting off encumbrances, paring down to the bare essentials, stripping for the journey. Possessions make me anxious. When Saul gave me my engagement ring, I worried for months. How would I hide it? For surely I should take it with me; I could sell it for food. But wouldn't it tempt bandits as I lay sleeping by the roadside? In their haste they might cut off my finger, and I carried no medical supplies. I was glad when times got hard and we had to sell the ring back to Arkin's Jewelers.

A husband was another encumbrance; I often thought that. And children even more so. (Not to mention their equipment: their sweaters, Band-Aids, stuffed animals, vitamins.) How did I end up with so much, when I had thrown so much away? I looked at my children with the same mixture of love and resentment that I used to feel for my Sleepy Doll. I would have liked to strip myself of people, too. I was pleased when I lost any friends.

My only important belonging since I have grown up is a pair of excellent walking shoes.

Nobody, of course, knew anything about this trip of mine, but often when I was thinking of it my mother complained that my eyes had turned flat. "I don't understand you," she used to say. "What makes you get that expression? It seems you've . . . folded up your *looks*, Charlotte. What's happened? You weren't always like this. Why, ever since, I don't know . . ."

Ever since my kidnapping, was what she meant. Except she didn't call it a kidnapping. She confused me. Sometimes she said I'd wandered to the midway out of contrariness; sometimes she said the fair people had maliciously lost me. Till I didn't really know any more: what had happened? What did it mean?

I had been kidnapped, I was almost certain, but when I tried to remember I was not so sure who had done it. I'd been kidnapped and placed on a dining room table, imprisoned in an eyelet dress; set on a splintery gold-painted throne; rushed through a field by a man in a leather jacket; hurried into a pickup truck by a fat lady who talked on and on: "I never had such a fright in my life. I thought we had lost you. Our only, single child, our little girl. I thought, 'How will we ever . . .' I thought you were dead, smothered maybe or strangled. You're so thin, it wouldn't take much to . . . you were thin even as a baby and I worried night and day over you. Thin as a stick. Thin as a wire. When they brought you to me I said, 'She's so thin!' You had this very straight dark hair, I had never seen so much hair on a baby. You had a forceps mark on your temple that stayed there till you were two years old. Remember, Murray? I said, 'What is that mark? *My* baby didn't have forceps, she slipped right out. The doctor told me so himself.' Oh, why don't they answer your questions?"

She let her hands fall into her lap. My father sighed. The two of them stared out at the night while the pickup rattled on, stealing me away.

5

We came to one of those city-type service stations, all fluorescent lights, scroungy blue-jeaned boy pumping gas, German shepherd in the plate glass window. Jake Simms walked slowly and kept looking it over, I didn't know what for. Then he said, "This'll do." He cut in across the concrete, pushing me ahead of him. "I got to go to the john," he said. "Got some other things to do besides. Ask the boy for the keys."

"What?"

"The keys, keys. Ask him for the keys to the john."

I asked. The boy was washing a windshield now and he stopped and listened, as if he couldn't do more than one thing at a time. His ruffled yellow head tilted toward me; his knuckles were soiled and leathery. "I want the key," I told him.

"*Keys!*" Jake hissed behind me.

"Both keys. One for him too."

The boy set his cloth aside and dug down in his jeans, which were so tight he had to suck in his breath before he could get a hand in his pocket. One key was attached to a huge metal washer, the other to a wooden disc. "Don't forget to give them back," the boy said.

"Sure thing," Jake told him.

We went around to the restrooms, where the doors were chained and padlocked, and he opened up the Ladies' and shoved me in. I was uncertain what was going on. Was this the end of the road? Was he planning to leave for good now? Till he said, "Don't go away," and shut the door on me. I heard the key turning, then his footsteps growing fainter. For a long time after he was gone the chain went on swinging against the door like a handful of marbles being thrown down, over and over again.

Well, of course I was glad to see the inside of a bathroom. I peed ten gallons, washed my hands, looked at my face in the speckled mirror. My hair was a little stringy but other than that I seemed the same as usual. Evidently these things don't show on a person the way you'd think they would.

But then I glanced up and saw how dim and tiny the ceiling was, hung with cobwebs—oh, this was a closed-in space, all right. One little window high up the cinderblock wall, chicken wire and milky glass, slanted partway open. I climbed onto the toilet seat. Standing on tiptoe, I could press my face to the window and see what little there was to see: a strip of blackness and the gleaming roofs of a few cars left overnight for repairs. Not a single human being, no one to get me out of there. Anybody would have been welcome, even Jake Simms. I was ready to rattle the windowpane like a prison grate and call his name. But then I saw him. He turned out to be a bent shape by one of the parked cars; he straightened and started toward me. I hopped down and slung my purse over my shoulder. When he opened the door I was just standing there, calm as you please. I didn't give a sign how nervous I had been.

"Over this way," he said.

He led me into the dark, toward the clump of cars I'd seen from the window. One car was long, humped—I didn't get a good look at it. On the passenger side the front door handle and the back door handle were looped through with a chain and padlocked. We edged between cars to get to the driver's side. Jake opened the door and pushed me onto the seat. "Slide over," he said.

I looked at him.

"Don't try no funny stuff, I got it locked with the men's room chain."

I slid over. Cars are closed-in spaces too, even without locked doors, and this one could smother a person, I thought, with its fuzzy, dusty-smelling seat covers and slit-eyed windows. There were no headrests. A pair of giant fur dominoes hung from the rear-view mirror. "What kind of car *is* this?" I asked.

"Beggars can't be choosers," said Jake. "None of them others had their keys left in."

He settled into the driver's seat and inched the door shut, so it barely clicked when it latched. Then he let his breath out and sat still a minute. "Question is, does it work," he told me.

I heard the rustle of nylon, a key turning. The engine came on with a grudging sound. Jake slipped into reverse, and I saw the car ahead of us sliding away. Since I'm not a driver myself, I went on facing forward. So it came as a shock when *wham!*—we hit something. I spun around but I couldn't see what it was. A mailbox, it sounded like. Something clattery. "Oh, hell," Jake said, and shifted gears and roared into the street. But even that didn't bring anybody out after us. At least, I was still looking backward and I didn't notice anyone.

"See, I didn't want to brake," Jake said. "Didn't want the brake lights lit."

But now that we were out of there and into the ordinary,

evening-time traffic, he switched on the headlights and settled back. I couldn't believe it. Was that *it?* Simple as that? "Well. My goodness," I said. "I never knew a life of crime could be so easy."

He looked at me sideways. He said, "A what? Life of what?"

I didn't answer (not wanting to get in any trouble). We rode along a ways. Turned right. Passed a line of people in front of a restaurant. Then, "Ha," he said. "Bet you think I'm some kind of a criminal, don't you."

"Um . . ."

"Think I'm a crook or something."

I decided it was best not to mention the bank robbery. I smoothed my skirt down and settled my purse on my lap. We turned left. Buildings grew sparser.

"That what you think?" he asked me.

"*I* don't know what you are and I don't care," I said.

He stopped for a traffic light. He was chewing on his lower lip; no wonder it got so chapped. When the light turned green the car started off with a jerk, as if suddenly reminded of something. The tires screamed, the dominoes bounced. "Fact is, I ride demolition derbies," said Jake.

I thought he was making a joke about his driving, but his face stayed serious. "I do a lot of them out roundabout," he said. "Hagerstown, Potomac . . . Maryland's just full of them."

"Full of . . . demolition derbies?"

"Last year, I won three. But generally I do a whole lot better."

"Well, I thought that was just a weekend thing, demolition derbies. You make your *living* doing that?"

"What I make is my affair," he said.

"I mean—"

"If I have to I'll hire on a few days in a body shop or something, but I don't really like doing nothing but them derbies. I am a demolition fool, I tell you. I like that better than eating. I never could go for that *soft* life, sitting around in some house, no way out, wife, kids, goldfish . . . I like to get my hands on, say, a good solid Ford, sixty-two or three or long about there, and just mow all them others flat. Run that thing into the ground. Finest feeling I know of."

He swerved for an animal carcass, not braking at all.

"Bet *you* thought I was some type of criminal," he told me.

"Well . . ."

"Want to know the truth?"

I waited. He shot his eyes over at me, shot them back. In the dark his face was hard to read. "Whole trouble is this: I'm a victim of impulse," he said.

"Of—?"

"Impulse."

"Oh."

"Buddy of mine told me that," he said. "Guy name of Oliver. Oliver Jamison. This real smart character I hooked up with in the training school when him and me was teenagers. See, *he* didn't care. If they was to lock him up, why, he'd just pull out a book and commence to reading, that was the type of a guy he was. Me, I like to go crazy if I am locked up. I mean it. I like to go crazy. I'll do anything I must to get away. You take that training school, I busted an ankle jumping out the chaplain's bathroom window there. I ran clear to the woods on a busted ankle. Only had a month left to go, too. That's when this Oliver says what he says. When they brung me back he says, 'Jake,' he says, 'you're a victim of impulse.' Thing stuck in my mind. 'You're a victim of impulse,' he says to me."

He turned onto a highway, some little two-lane thing leaving the city. The engine made a snarling sound. "People who hold the power are the ones that don't mind locks," Jake said. "Now, Oliver, he was pretty cool. I liked that Oliver. I would call him O.J. He had this interest in blowing things up. I mean kid stuff—bombs in mailboxes. He would make the bombs by hand. He sure was smart. After they taken a look at the damage this chemical company offered him a scholarship, but he turned it down. Well, I get his point. See, mailboxes, there's a real satisfaction to a mailbox. But you don't want to go to work for no chemical company."

A driver heading toward us flashed his lights, no doubt so Jake would lower his beams, but Jake didn't seem to notice.

"What I told him was, 'It's circumstances somewhat too. It ain't entirely impulse,' I'd say. I mean you take this afternoon, for instance. Take a while back. Accidents, bad timing, dumb guy pulling a piece . . . you get what I mean? I lack good luck. I am not a lucky man."

"Well, I don't understand how you can say that," I told him.

"Huh?"

"What if this car hadn't started, for instance? Back at the service station. It *was* in for repairs, remember. What if it hadn't started after you'd gone and chained the . . . and what if there'd been no key? Lots of places take better care than that, they keep the keys in the cash register or something. Or if the boy had been standing outside, what then?"

"Why, I would get a car from somewheres else," Jake said.

"But—"

"Like, you could go to a snorkel box. Ever hear of that? Snorkel mailbox. Jam the slot so a letter don't properly fall inside it. Guy drives up in his car, tries to stuff a letter through, gets out to see what went wrong. Leaving his key in of course and engine running, door wide open. All you got to do is hop in. Simple. See?"

"But then he would know right away," I said. "He could be after you so fast."

"Now, there you got it," Jake said. He snapped his fingers. "You caught it straight off. I wouldn't never choose that method if I had other ways open to me."

"Right," I said, and then remembered. "Yes, but what I mean is, how can you say you're not lucky when it all went off so well?"

He turned. I could feel him staring at me. He said, "Lucky? Is that what you call it? When some fool turns up armed and a camera flips on and you get this lady on your hands you never bargained for, it's *lucky?*"

"Well . . ."

"It's circumstances, working against me," said Jake. "Like I told Oliver: I surely don't plan it like this. Events get out of my control. But Oliver, oh, he could be such a smart-ass. 'Your whole life is out of your control,' that's what Oliver said. 'Your whole life.' Smart-ass."

I don't know what time it was when we stopped. Around ten, maybe. We had been traveling through that deep, country dark that makes you feel too thin. The road was so raspy and patched, with so many curves, crossroads, stop signs—I kept nodding off to sleep, but every bump jarred my mind up to the surface again and I never really forgot where I was. So when we stopped I was awake in an instant, on guard. "What's wrong?" I said.

"Durn motor quit."

He flicked on the inside light, which made my eyes squinch up. "I knew from the start something like this was bound to happen," he told me.

"Maybe it's out of gas."

He peered at the gas meter. He tapped it.

"Is that what it is?"

I could tell it was; he wouldn't look at me. He got out of

the car and said, "You steer, I'm going to push her to the side of the road."

"But I don't drive," I told him.

"What's that got to do with it? Just steer, is all I ask. Move over and steer."

He slammed the door shut. I moved over. A second later I felt his weight against the back of the car, inching it forward, and I steered as best I could though it was hard to see much with the inside light on. I guided it a few feet down the road, wondering what I would do if the engine roared up and took off. Freedom! I would leave him far behind, head for the nearest highway. Except that I really couldn't drive at all and had just the vaguest notion where the brake pedal was. So I steered to the right, finally, onto a strip of dirt so narrow that some kind of scratchy bushes tore at the side of the car. I heard Jake give a yell. The car stopped. When he came around and opened the door he said, "Now there was no call whatsoever to run her on into the woods."

"Well, I told you I couldn't drive."

He sighed. He reached in to turn off the lights; then he said, "Okay, come on."

"What are we doing now?"

"Going to head for that service station we passed a ways back."

"Maybe I could just sit here and wait for you," I said.

"Ha."

I climbed out of the car. My legs felt stiff, and it seemed my shoes had hardened into some shape that didn't fit me. "Is it far?" I asked.

"Not too."

We started walking—smack down the middle of the road, for there was no car in either direction. He had hold of my arm again in the same sore place as before. His hand felt small and wiry. "Listen," I said, "can't you let me walk on my own? Where would I run to, anyway?"

He didn't answer. Nor did he let go of me.

The air had a damp smell, as if it might rain, and seemed warmer than what I was used to. At least, I wasn't shivering any more. From the little I could see, I guessed we were traveling through farm country. Once we passed a barn, and then a shed with the sleepy clucking of hens inside it. "Where on earth *are* we?" I asked.

"How would I know? Virginia, somewheres."

"My feet hurt."

"It don't make sense that you can't drive a car," he said, as if that were to blame for all our troubles. "That's about the dumbest thing I ever heard of."

"What's dumb about it?" I asked him. "Some people drive, some people don't. It just so happens I'm one of them that don't."

"Only a whiffle-head would not know how to drive," said Jake. "That's how I look at it." He wiped his face on his sleeve. We walked on. We rounded a curve that I had some hopes for, but on the other side there was only more darkness.

"I thought you said it wasn't far," I said.

"It ain't."

"I feel like my feet are dropping off."

"Just hold the phone, we'll get there by and by."

"My toes ache clear to my kneecaps."

"Will you quit that? Geeze, you'd think that guy could've filled his gas tank once in a while."

"Maybe he didn't know how long you'd be stealing it for," I said.

He said, "Watch yourself, lady."

I decided to watch myself.

Around the next curve was the filling station, such as it was: one dimly lit sign, two pumps, and a lopsided shack. As soon as we saw it, Jake let go of my arm. "Now, pay attention," he said. "You're going to ask the guy for a can of gas. You got that?"

"Well, how come *I* always have to ask for things?" I said.

Something jabbed me in the small of the back: the gun. Oh, Lord, the gun, which I had thought we were through with, and in fact had let slip my mind as if it never existed. That prodding black nubbin in the hand of a victim of impulse. I crossed the road and climbed the cinderblock steps, with Jake close behind me. I opened the warped wooden door. For a moment all I saw was a pyramid of PennZoil tins, a faded calendar girl in a one-piece latex swimsuit, and stacks of looseleaf auto-parts catalogues. Then I found an old man in a wicker chair. He was watching TV with the sound turned off. "Evening," he said, not looking around.

"Good evening."

"Something I can do for you folks?"

"Well, our car ran out of gas and I . . . we need a can of . . ."

"Fine, just fine," said the old man, and he went on watching TV. There was a commercial on, someone holding up a bottle and silently rejoicing. Then a news announcer appeared at a bare, artificial-looking desk, and the old man sighed and stood up. "A tin," he said. "Tin." He went rummaging behind a stack of tires in one corner, but came up with nothing. "Wait a minute," he said, and went outside. As soon as he was gone, Jake pushed me further into the room and leaned over to turn up the sound on the TV. ". . . with no end in sight," the announcer said, "though experts predict that by mid-summer there may well be a . . ."

Jake switched channels. He traveled through a lady shampooing her hair, a man making a speech, a man playing golf. He arrived at another news announcer, pale and snowy. "Traffic on the Bay Bridge this summer is expected to reach an all-time high," this announcer said from a distance. Jake turned up the sound. The man grew louder but no clearer, and sadly shuffled his papers as if he realized it. A picture appeared of Jake and me, backing away from the camera. In spite of the snow, our faces seemed more distinct now. By next week you would be able to count our eyelashes, maybe even read our thoughts. But our stay was much briefer this time, cut off in midstep. We were replaced by my husband, a towering hatrack of a man, gaunt and cavernous and haunted-looking as always, sitting on our flowered sofa. I felt something tearing inside me. "That bank robbery in Clarion," the announcer said, "is not yet solved, and police are concerned about a woman hostage who has been identified as Mrs. Charlotte Emory."

My husband vanished. A picture teetered up of me alone, photographed by my father for my high school graduation: my fifties self with lacquered hairdo, cowgirl scarf, and cheeky black smile. Then Saul returned. The announcer said, "Our own Gary Schneider talked with her husband this evening for 'Views on News' cameras."

Gary Schneider, who wasn't pictured, asked something I didn't catch. Saul stopped cracking his knuckles. He said, "Yes, naturally I'm worried, but I have faith she'll be returned to us. The police believe that the bandit is still in this area."

His voice was hollow. He didn't seem to be thinking of what he was saying.

"Would you care to comment, sir," said Gary Schneider, "on that sidewalk witness who said they appeared to be running away *together*? Do you have any feeling that this may have been a voluntary action on her part?"

"That's ridiculous," said Saul, and he straightened slowly and took on a looming, ominous appearance that caused Gary Schneider to say, "Uh, well, I just—"

"Charlotte wouldn't do such a thing. She's a good woman, really, it's just that . . . and I know she would never leave me."

Something clanked. Jake spun around. The old man stood there with a gasoline can, shaking his head at the TV. "How long *you* been watching?" Jake asked—so mean you couldn't miss it, but the old man only smiled.

"Why, I was one of the first in this valley to purchase a set," he said. "This here is my third; run clear through the other two. Matter of fact I been thinking of color but I'm scared of the cancer rays."

"Yeah, well," said Jake.

He paid him for the gas and the can. The old man said he would trust us for the can, but Jake said, "Might as well do like I'm used to," and handed over the money and took the can and nudged me out the door. When we left, the old man was already stooped before the TV trying to get his favorite channel back.

As soon as we were outside again, Jake said, "You told me you were leaving your husband."

"I was," I said.

"How come he said what he did, then? You lied."

"*He* lied," I said. "*I* don't know why he said that. Not only was I planning to leave him but I've left before, and he knows it. Back in nineteen sixty. And I told him I would in sixty-eight also as well as a lot of other times, I couldn't say just when, exactly..."

"Oh, hell, I might have known," said Jake.

"Now, what is that supposed to mean?"

But he wouldn't answer. We walked on, our feet luffing softly on the scabby highway. The air felt chillier and a fine cold spray had started up.

Oh, I certainly would have liked to give that Saul a piece of my mind. He was always doing things like that. Always saying, "I'm certain you won't leave me, Charlotte." I just wished he could see me now. I wished I could mail him a postcard: "Having wonderful time, moving on at last, love to all." From Florida, or the Bahamas, or the Riviera.

But then I stepped in some sort of pothole and cold water

splashed to my knees, and my shoes started leaking as if they were no more than paper, and we rounded a curve and came upon the car: hulking in the dark, tilting off the side of the road like a lame man. When we reached it, Jake opened the door and snaked an arm inside to turn the lights on. The headlights flared up, but the ceiling light wavered and died. "Why!" I said (for up till now I hadn't taken a really good look). "Why, what *is* this?"

"Huh?" said Jake. He set the can down and unscrewed the cap of the gas tank.

"Why, it's a—some kind of *antique*," I said.

"Sure. Fifty-three, would be my guess."

"But—" I said. I stepped back, peering at the toothy grille, the separate bumper like a child's orthodontic appliance. The long, bulbous body was streaked with chrome in unexpected places. Over the headlights there were visors as coy as eyelashes, and the lights themselves had a peculiar color, I thought—dull orange, and cloudy. "It'll stick out a mile!" I said. "Everyone will notice. It will catch people's eyes like . . . for goodness sake," I said.

Gas burbled into the tank, on and on.

"This is just plain stupid," I said.

The can landed far away, in bushes or branches or something crackly. "Get in," Jake told me.

I got in. He climbed in after me and slammed the door. The motor started up with a cough, and when we pulled onto the road we bounced and swayed on our squeaky springs. I let my head loll back against the seat and closed my eyes.

"Well, there's one thing," I heard Jake say. "You're shed of that Frankenstein husband at least and that cruddy flowered sofa. Shed of that spooky little old lamp with the beads hanging off it. Oh, you couldn't keep *me* shut in no boring house. Ought to be glad you're out of it. Any day now, you're going to be thanking me. Is how *I* look at it."

But that's the only lamp we have, I wanted to say. I've given the others away. I've given the rugs away too and the curtains and most of the furniture. How much more can I get rid of? My head was growing heavy, though, and my eyes wouldn't open. I fell asleep.

6

I dreamed about my husband, but he was younger and lacked those two vertical hollows in his cheeks. He had on a crewneck sweater I'd forgotten he ever owned. His trousers were khaki, like the Army pants he wore while we were dating. The sight of him made me sad.

My husband was the boy next door, but to tell the truth we didn't grow up together. He was several years older than I was—old enough to make a difference, back in school. When I was in eighth grade he was a senior, one of the Emory boys, long-boned and lazy, up to no good. Anyone could tell you who Saul Emory was. While I was just getting my bearings, in those days. I still looked like a child. I'd been systematically starving myself ever since I'd discovered my breasts (two little pillows of fat, like my mother's chins), and you could see the blue veins in my temples and the finest details of articulation in my wrists and knees and elbows. I had a posture problem and no one could figure out what to do with my hair.

Saul Emory graduated and went away, and I moved on through the years until I was a senior myself, and secretary of the student body and first runner-up for Homecoming Queen. I had come into my own, by then. I deserved to; I worked so hard at it. The one thing I wanted most of all was for people to think that I was normal.

Through an enormous effort of will, I became known as the most vivacious girl in the senior class. Also best-groomed, with my Desert Flower cologne and my noose of Poppit pearls, and my Paint the Town Pink lipstick refreshed in the restroom hourly with a feathery little brush like the ones the models used. I had a few boyfriends, though nobody serious. And girl-friends too; we rolled each other's hair up at I don't know how many slumber parties. I never gave a slumber party myself, of course. No one ever asked me why not.

I would stay after school for sorority meetings, Honor Society, Prom Committee, cheerleading . . . but those things can only last so long. In the end I would find myself home again, walking into the overused air and my parents' eternal questions: Why hadn't I said goodbye that morning? What had kept me so late? Who was the boy who drove me home? And would I be staying in tonight, for once?

Then I would look down at them (for I was taller than both, by now) and everything came back to me: I remembered who I really was. In the smoky mirror behind my mother, my pearls were as outlandish as a string of bear claws. My face had a yellowed look around the edges.

I graduated from high school and got a part scholarship in mathematics at Markson College, over in Holgate. It seemed too simple. I kept wondering where the catch was.

Yet the day after Labor Day, there I sat in my father's

pickup with my suitcases piled in the rear. My mother didn't come with us; it was hard for her to travel. As I waved to her out the window I had a sudden worry that she knew how glad I was that she was staying home. I wondered if that were *why* she was staying home. I waved all the harder, blew kisses. This was one time I didn't try to get out of saying goodbye.

Then my father drove me to Markson College, started to speak but gave up in the end, and left me at the dormitory. I was almost the first one there because I'd been so anxious to arrive. My roommate hadn't come yet, whoever she was. It was noon but the cafeteria didn't open till suppertime, so I ate an apple I'd brought and some Fig Newtons that my mother had tucked in my suitcase. The Fig Newtons made me unexpectedly homesick. Each bite caused my chest to ache. I had to hide them away in a drawer, finally. Then I unpacked, and put sheets on one bed, and wandered up and down the hall a while peeking into deserted rooms. After that I spent half an hour sitting at my desk, looking out the window at an empty sky. I'd brought along some curtains, but wasn't going to hang them till my roommate approved them. However, time was creeping. I decided I'd hang them anyway. I unfolded the curtains, took off my shoes, and climbed onto a radiator. Spread-eagled against the window, I chanced to look down at the quadrangle. And there was my fat cousin Clarence, lumbering toward my dormitory in that ponderous, tilting way he had.

I had known all along that escape couldn't be so easy.

My father was in the hospital. He had had an accident while driving home. The doctors weren't so much worried about his injuries as about the heart attack that had caused the accident in the first place. Or maybe the accident had caused the heart attack. I don't think they ever did get it straight.

For three weeks we stayed near his bed—Mama in her wooden lawn chair that Clarence had brought from home and me in an easy chair. We watched my father's face, which looked queer in horizontal position. His skin around his eyes had gone all crumpled. It tired him even to say a few words. Mostly he slept, and my mother cried, and I sat willing him awake again so that I could get to know him. I couldn't stand to think how I had let him slide through my life all these years. I made a lot of promises; you know the kind. I brought my mother tea and glazed doughnuts, the only things that would sit on her stomach. I dealt with the doctors and nurses. I tried reading various women's magazines, but all that talk about make-up and weight control and other frills just made me sick. I don't remember eating any food whatsoever, though I suppose I must have.

Then they let him go home, but only by ambulance. We fixed a bed in his studio and laid him flat upon it. His face lost a little of its chalkiness. He started acting more natural, fussing at the itchy tape they had bound his broken ribs with. It worried him that customers were being turned away. "Charlotte," he said, "you know how to handle that camera. I want you to do it for a week or so, just till I'm back on my feet. Can you manage?"

I said yes. I was numb by then. Now that he was safe it had hit me finally where I was: home, trapped, no escape. My mother couldn't even sit him up without me there to help. I saw my life rolling out in front of me like an endless, mildewed rug.

It seemed to me that photos froze a person, pinned him to cardboard like a butterfly. Why would anyone want them? But people did, apparently. Poor-white mothers in rayon shifts, holding overdressed babies. Soldiers with their arms around their skinny, frizzy-haired girlfriends. I took their pictures indifferently. The camera was old and clumsy; almost anything you did to it had to take place in the dark. But I'd been using it most of my life, and couldn't see why my father became so anxious and critical all of a sudden. "Move that lamp off somewhat," he would tell me from his bed. "You don't want such a glare. Now get yourself more of an angle. I never did like a head-on photograph."

What he liked was a sideways look—eyes lowered, face slanted downward. The bay window displaying my father's portraits resembled a field full of flowers, all being blown by the same strong breeze.

In the darkroom (a walk-in closet, remodeled) I had attacks of shortness of breath. I would grit my teeth and endure, meanwhile developing prints with the sensible half of my mind. Everything about that place was depressed: cluttered or leaking or peeling. All the labels had come off the bottles of chemicals. Nothing was where it was supposed to be. It seemed my father didn't care any more than I did.

But you would never guess that from the way he acted. Fuss, fuss. Questioning every little thing I did. When it came time to show him any prints he would have me hang them on the clothesline near his bed. Then there'd be this long, disapproving silence while he lay frowning and pinching his mustache. "Oh, well," he'd finally say, "most of these people have got no judgment anyway." Yet I didn't think I'd done so badly. In fact I think a lot of the customers preferred me to my father. My father had such set ideas, for one thing. He still photographed children against that Ionic column of his. Me, I would take a picture any way people asked. I had no feelings about it.

We lived in a smaller and smaller area of the house, now —shutting off floors my father couldn't climb to, rooms we couldn't afford to heat. Our neighborhood had narrowed too. The pickup was on cinderblocks out back, and anyway neither Mama nor I could drive, so we did all our shopping on foot. And nobody came to visit us. The Emorys next door had moved away by then; the other neighbors thought we were peculiar. All my friends were in college or married, divided from me forever after. It got so I would welcome the most random customers like long-lost relatives. But I saw how oddly they looked at us. I knew the picture we made: fat mother in elastic stockings, shriveled father, sullen spinster daughter. House where everything was mislaid under something else, and bats were surely hanging in the turret.

Markson College sent me a letter saying I could enter in January, if I liked. I don't know what I'd been hoping—maybe for them to close the school completely till I could get there. But they didn't even tell me who my roommate was, and I guessed anyway that she'd found somebody else by now. I felt nothing would ever go right for me again. Every customer standing on his head in my camera seemed happier than I was.

By December, the doctors said my father could start getting up. His first piece of action was to take my photographs off the clothesline and set out some of his own. You could tell he'd been just itching to do that. He stood there in his corduroy slippers, with his sweater tucked accidentally into his trousers, pointing to photos he had taken twenty years ago. "Now, here is a fine . . . this was a very important man as I recall, rose high in the county government later on in life. I believe he came to me because I take an honest portrait. You see, Charlotte, I never have held with these fancied-*up* photographs. No sense pretending someone is what he isn't."

His clothes swallowed him; his gray hair had taken on a tobacco tint and his skin was loose and sagging. But I couldn't get him to rest a while. He pulled out more and more photos, tacking them to the bulletin board, propping them on shelves and along the picture rails. Businessmen, high school graduates, ladies' circles from the old days, thinning out to the soldiers and the overdressed babies. But even the babies looked serious in these pictures, and the soldiers stood stiff as family men beside their girls. Everyone's expression was bemused and veiled; everyone's posture was perfect. Nobody smiled. I hadn't noticed that before. I said, "Look! It's like some old-fashioned photo album."

"It is never old-fashioned to take an honest portrait," my father said.

I was afraid he was working up to one of his moods. I saw now that he was hanging new prints too fast, not even looking at them, hauling out more and more from the rusty green file beside his bed. "See, here is a . . . this was . . . this man ordered forty prints from me, that's how much he liked what I did."

"It's very nice, Daddy," I said. I just wanted him to stop moving around so much. I didn't care two cents about anybody's photos, his or mine either one. I said, "Shouldn't you be resting now?"

"Ask your mother what she did with those old plates of mine," he told me.

I went to find my mother, who was watching TV in her lawn chair in the kitchen. "Daddy wants his old negatives," I said.

"What negatives? Why ask me? I don't know why he keeps all that stuff anyway," she said. "They sit around cracking under their own weight, by and by. And you know those people aren't going to reorder, most of them are dead now."

I went back to the studio. "She hasn't seen them," I said. My father was sorting a shoebox full of church groups. From the look he gave me, you would think I'd lost his negatives myself. I didn't know why he was so angry with me.

That night I dreamed I went to Markson College and found it locked and abandoned, its quadrangles echoing; but after I woke up I felt all right again. I put on my bathrobe and went down to the kitchen to start the coffee. While it was perking I looked out the window at the sun coming up through a tangle of frosty trees. Then I poured two cups of coffee, one for me and one for my father, and carried them into the studio. My father lay in bed under a perfectly smooth blanket. He wasn't breathing. All around him and above him were pictures of unsmiling people, but none was any stiller than my father was.

Uncle Gerard saw to the funeral. Then he and Aunt Aster attended it (I don't know who else, if anyone) while I stayed home with my mother, who was going to pieces. I thought of it as going to pieces because she seemed to be taking everything else to pieces right along with her. She would sit in her chair and pluck, pluck at the cushion till little bits of stuffing were scattered all over the rug. She would pick the houseplants purely bald and roll each leaf and shred it up. Sometimes she ran her fingers dreamily through her hair and pulled out strands, one by one. I didn't know what to do with her. All I could think of was to hold her hands and say, "Stop, now."

"I always guessed that this was going to happen," she told me. Her voice had lost its tone. You can't imagine how scary it is to hear someone just printing out words like that. "This was the one thing I always dreaded," she said, "and now it's come, I've been left without a husband forever."

It seemed to me that she ought to be relieved, then. She had nothing more to dread. But of course I didn't say so out loud. I patted her arm. Fetched her tea. And went to my uncle's as soon as she had fallen asleep. I was desperate; January was just around the corner. "Uncle Gerard, I have got to go to college," I told him.

"College?" he said, and lit one of his terrible-smelling black cigars.

"They gave me just a part scholarship and you know we're short on money. I'll have to ask you for a loan."

"Well, money, sweetheart, certainly," said Uncle Gerard, "but what're you going to do about your mama?"

"I can't stay with Mama all my life."

"Why, girl! She's *stricken*. You want to leave her at a time like this?"

"Maybe she could move in with you," I said.

"With *Aster* and me?"

"Or maybe you could just look in on her from time to time. Or send Clarence over. I mean, just to—"

"Now, here is what I would suggest," said Uncle Gerard, and he braced his hands on his stubby thighs and leaned toward me, breathing burnt rubber. "You're, what. Seventeen? Eighteen? Look at you, got all the time in the world. Take a year out. Start school next fall. What's a year to somebody your age?"

"It's one-eighteenth of my life," I said.

"And I tell you what I'm going to do: you wait till next September and I'll pay your bills myself. Outright. No loans. It's a deal, you got that?"

"Well, thank you, Uncle Gerard," I said, because I could see he meant well. He wasn't really so rich, after all; he owned a dry-cleaning establishment. But when I left I couldn't bring myself to say goodbye to Aunt Aster, with her golden hair and her pampered skin. I pretended not to hear her when she called to me from the kitchen.

Mama was not improving. In fact I wondered if even September would be long enough. I felt locked in a calendar; time was turning out to be the most closed-in space of all. I had to help Mama into her clothes every day and tell her things over and over. All she would talk about was my father. "I married him out of desperation," she told me. "I settled for what I could get. Don't ever *settle,* Charlotte."

"No, Mama."

She didn't have to tell me that.

"From the beginning, he held something against me. I still don't know what it was. He liked a hefty woman, he said, but after a while he started nagging for me to cut down on my eating. 'How come?' I asked him. I was so surprised that he would be like that. But I tried, oh, for his sake I . . . all those times I went without meals, and got weak and dizzy just trying to reduce some. Then, I don't know, I would have to start eating again. I'm just made that way, I just need more nourishment than other people. Oh, and it wouldn't have changed things anyhow. He wasn't a satisfied man, Charlotte. What more could I have done?"

"I don't know, Mama."

"Do you think he felt *he* had settled?"

"Of course not, Mama."

"He said it, all the time. 'Oh, why am I stuck in this *life*,' he said, and then I said, 'Go, go, who asked you to stay? Go someplace else if you don't like it here. Marry some floozy,' I told him; but he would just look at me from under his eyebrows and not say another word. 'I'll find you a bride *myself!*' I said. Yet it would have killed me, Charlotte. Isn't that comical? Laugh. He had the softest, saddest expression. He had this way of tipping his head when he listened to people. Oh, Charlotte, was he happy at all, do you think?"

"Of course he was, Mama," I said, and then I would have to leave, I just had to. I would go to the studio where my father's photographs still averted their eyes and his dented metal sign still swung outside the window: AMES STUDIOS. FINE PORTRAITS. Sometimes people came and rang at the outer entrance and I would let them in, for lack of anything better to do. I would take whatever pictures they asked. "Could you do my poodle? He's old and we want a memento in case he passes on." I could feel my father wince. But I won't say it really bothered me and, besides, we needed the money.

We made barely enough to keep us fed, that winter. Uncle Gerard slipped us ten-dollar bills from time to time but that just paid for Mama's blood pressure medicine. Finally in desperation I put up a ROOMS TO LET sign, and a factory watchman named Mr. Robb took the east front bedroom. He didn't like it much, though. He said we kept the house too cold, and he moved out three weeks later. The sign just gathered dust. I tried a little harder in the studio and asked all customers if they would tell their friends about us, but that didn't help. I think the sight of Mama put them off. She had this way of wandering in sometimes, halfway through a sitting—pulling herself along by clutching at pieces of furniture. I could tell when she was coming by the sudden startled look on a customer's face. "It's amazing," she would say in the doorway, "how every corner of the world agrees simultaneously that someone's dead. Don't you think so? I mean if a man dies in one room then his meal in another room goes untouched; he doesn't show up for his doctor appointment; the photos he was sorting just stay in a heap. There's never a slip-up; the world has everything so well arranged."

"My mother," I would tell the customer. "Look a little toward the light, please."

"But then I never did place much faith in physical things," said my mother. "Oftentimes I've set a cup down and left it somewhere, and been surprised to see it there two weeks later. You would think just once there'd be a lapse of some kind; the cup would forget and be back on the shelf when I looked at it again. Or gravity: you'd think you could take gravity by surprise, just once, and set a tray very suddenly on air and have it stay. Wouldn't you?"

The customer would clear his throat.

"I see now I didn't give the world enough credit," my mother said, and then she wandered out again.

On certain evil days I had thoughts of running away, but of course I never did.

One afternoon in late March, the front bell rang and I opened the door to a very tall soldier with his cap in his hand. He had straight black hair and that sealed kind of face that keeps its own counsel. An Emory face. Only I wasn't sure which one. I said, "Amos?"

"Saul," he told me.

"Saul!"

"Hello, Charlotte."

He didn't smile. (Emorys seldom do; they just look peaceful.) "I saw your sign," he said. "I came to town to settle the property and I wondered if I could room and board with you till I get it taken care of."

"Of course," I said. "We'd be glad to have you."

"I hear you've had some trouble this winter."

"Well, some," I said.

Saul only nodded. The Emorys were used to trouble; they didn't have to make a big to-do about it.

The way we knew the Emorys was this: the mother, Alberta, was a woman who kept no secrets. She would tell her business to anyone, even us. She would bring us a pie or a bowl of fresh berries and stand half the morning in our kitchen doorway, talking on and on in her lush soft voice. Discussing her husband, Edwin Emory the radio repairman, who drank far more than he worked. And her four strapping sons: Amos, Saul, Linus, and Julian. Julian was my age; the others were older. The men in that family were wicked and mysterious, but thanks to Alberta we always knew what they were up to. Amos kept running away; Saul got in trouble with girls a lot. Linus was subject to unexplainable rages and Julian had a tendency to gamble. I don't believe there was a day in their lives that something complicated wasn't happening to them.

This Alberta was a gypsyish type, beautiful in certain lights and carelessly dressed, slouchy, surprisingly young. In the summer she often went barefoot. Needless to say, I loved her. I hung on everything she told me: "Then what? Then what?" I wished she would adopt me. I longed for her teeming house and remarkable troubles. For on Alberta, troubles sat like riches. "Look," she seemed to be saying, "at how important my life is. See how I've been blessed with eventfulness?" And she would lift her warm brown hands, spilling wealth.

"She's got no common sense, that woman," my mother said.

I think what Mama meant was, sense to realize when she was badly off. Mama might have liked her better if Alberta would only come crying sometime. But Alberta never cried. She told her news between breaths of laughter: scandals, disasters, miracles, mysteries. Someone broke into the radio shop and wiped it out, left a note behind: "Sorry for the inconvenience." In Julian's handwriting. Her father-in-law arrived on the doorstep with all his worldly goods, sixty years' worth of clippings and old theatrical costumes, and since there were no extra bedrooms he slept in the dining room surrounded by fake ermine mantles, military uniforms, swords and crowns and boxes of hats. At any hour of the day or night he would call to her for health food snacks.

"That house ought to be boarded up and condemned," my mother said.

The winter of my junior year in high school, Alberta eloped with her father-in-law.

Well, it wasn't exactly your everyday occurrence. Edwin Emory staggered around looking stunned, but no more stunned than I was. I couldn't understand why she'd left them that way. (Left *me*.) I had thought she was so happy. But then, I also used to think that barbershop quartets on the radio were one man with a hoarse voice. What I mean to say is, I was easily fooled by appearances. Maybe all families, even the most normal-looking, were as queer as ours once you got up close to them. Maybe Alberta was secretly as sad as my mother. Or maybe, as Mama said, "That woman just wanted to be envied for everything, even her scruffy old father-in-law." I never had looked at it that way before.

For a while I brought the Emorys cookies and casseroles, but I never got much response. Their house sank in on itself and went silent. Edwin sat around drinking muscatel wine in his thermal underwear while Linus tried to run the shop. (Saul and Amos had left home years ago.) But mechanical things were depressing to Linus, and he had some kind of nervous breakdown and was sent to live with an aunt. Then Julian dropped out of school. He had a fight about a gambling debt and wasn't heard from again. And last of all, Edwin left. We didn't know exactly when, or for where. He just wasn't around any more. One day I chanced to look out the window and see a stranger boarding up the Emory house, just as Mama had always said they should. And that was the end of that.

Or seemed to be, till Saul came home. Saul wore a uniform so crisp it looked metallic; he stood in a room as if planted there. It was clear the Emorys hadn't dwindled away to nothing just because I had lost sight of them. Though he couldn't say exactly where a couple of his brothers were, he knew they were all alive—even Julian. And Alberta and her father-in-law were someplace in California, or had been as of last Christmas; not that Saul cared. Only Edwin was gone forever. He'd died of liver trouble while visiting his sister in New Jersey. Now Amoco was going to buy the house and tear it down for a filling station, beat out Texaco, and Saul was here to settle the sale and put the money into back taxes. He wanted to sell the radio shop as well. He would take the first offer, sign the papers, and go, he said. He'd just got out of the Army, had a life to start. He couldn't afford to spend much time on this.

But he did. The settling of the house took longer than he'd expected—you *know* how complicated just the title search could get, with Emorys—and then a broken-down radio shop is not all that much in demand. He stayed on through March, April. I was glad. With Saul around, life seemed more definite. We had to get on a schedule, give him his meals at predictable hours. Also, he was good at fixing things and he made repairs we'd been needing for years. In the evenings, he watched TV with me and Mama (who wouldn't say boo to him, in spite of his careful manners) or he took me out. We went to movies, or restaurants, or the B & B Soda Shop. He acted like a brother, never so much as held my hand, but there was a measuring look in his eyes. I didn't know what he was waiting for. At the end of an evening I would climb to my bedroom, and there in the mirror was this college-age girl in a sweater and skirt—not a sullen old spinster after all.

Well, of course I fell in love with him. How could I avoid it? With that serene, pure face of his, those heavy-lidded eyes. It hit me for maybe the first time in my life that someone could have a whole world inside his head that I would never guess at. I was desperate to know what he thought about things. What was it like to have a family like his, a mother like Alberta? How did he feel passing his house now, with the shutters sagging off their hinges? He never said. I couldn't ask. Every time I saw him I *wanted* to ask, but I had such a sense of his separateness that it didn't seem possible. We stayed locked in this friendly small talk about mortgage assumptions and leaky faucets. The real conversation was carried on in silence: he helped me into my sweater as if wrapping a breakable gift. He somehow knew to lift my hair and settle it over my collar in just the right way. And I threw out three bowls of batter, trying to make Alberta's buckwheat pancakes. Even my mother took part in this conversation, for when we were all together now she grew stiff and still. She sent us little rodenty glances. The three of us were strung on elastic, and not a person could move without joggling the others.

Then one night in April we were coming home from a movie, Lana Turner in something or other. We happened to walk past his father's radio shop. A narrow, dismal wooden place set between a sandwich joint and a shoe repair, vacant all this time, black as a toothless mouth. I could have cried just looking at it, so how must Saul have felt? I reached out and touched his arm, and instantly he stopped and took hold of my hand and looked down at me. "Listen," he said.

He scared me. I thought he was mad that I had touched

him; I'd upset the balance, some way. But what he said was, "You know I don't have a job yet, Charlotte."

I said, "Job?"

"And I don't seem to have any interests. I don't know what I'm going to do in life. So I'm waiting to see what just *lands*, but so far nothing has."

I couldn't tell what he was getting at. I said, "Um—"

"It's you and me I'm talking about, Charlotte."

"Oh," I said.

"I feel I have to have some kind of a future before I can say anything to you."

I still didn't understand. It seemed like an excuse, to tell the truth. I was used to high school dates, where the future had no bearing whatsoever. "Well," I said, "is that all you're waiting for? I like you better without a future."

But I might as well not have spoken, because his face stayed troubled the rest of the walk home. Though he did keep hold of my hand, and on our front porch he kissed me—but only once, and very gravely, like somebody much, much older than me. Which he was, in a way. I was so young! I didn't think ahead at all. I only thought how strange it felt to touch surfaces like this, from behind our two private selves. I could have stood there all night with my head against his woolen shoulder. It was Saul who finally said we should go in.

My mother started condensing somehow, shrinking and drying. She was scared. I saw how she watched Saul with her bright, webbed eyes. The kinder he was to her, the more carefully she watched him. When he asked her a question it took her a long time to answer; she had to rise up through so many layers of fear. At night, when I helped her into bed, she clutched my wrist hard and peered into my face and moved her lips but said nothing. Then I would go downstairs and Saul would grip that very same wrist and draw me toward him. For a second I always felt confused and panicky. "What is it?" he would ask me, but I never told.

I kept trying to understand him. It wasn't easy. He lacked the recklessness that I had expected of him—had hoped of him, even. If anything, he was too serious. (When I was in high school, they always told you to look for a sense of humor.) He treated me in a stern, unsmiling way that made me shy. Also, I couldn't figure out this job business. It seemed he was waiting for his life's work to be issued like a fate. Really, he was so trustful. "Maybe you ought to just set out and seek your fortune," I said, only half joking. "That's what *I* would do. Oh, I'd love to go with you! Take off tomorrow, travel anywhere."

"No, you wouldn't," he said. "Leave your mother? At this point in her life?"

I don't know how a man like that could have been a son of Alberta's.

In May, he bought me an engagement ring. He took it out of his pocket one night when the three of us were eating supper —a little diamond. I hadn't known anything about it. I just stared at him when he slipped it on my finger.

"I thought it was time," he told me. "I'm sorry, Mrs. Ames," he said. "I can't wait any longer, I want to marry her."

Mama said, "But I—"

"It won't be right away," he said. "I'm not taking her off tomorrow. I don't even know what my work will be yet. We'll stay here as long as you need us, believe me. I promise you."

"But—" Mama said.

That was all, though.

I should have refused. I wasn't helpless, after all. I should have said, "I'm sorry, I can't fit you in. I never planned to take a second person on this trip." But I didn't. He was sitting next to me, and the leathery, foreign smell of his skin called up so much love that I seemed to be damaged by it. Everything he said was peculiarly clear, as if spoken in crackling cold air. It really didn't occur to me to turn him down.

$$\boxed{7}$$

I woke with a sense of being rocked and shaken. I sat up and looked around me. The sun was so bright it made my eyes ache, but I could see that we were parked in a marshy, straw-colored field. Jake was at the wheel, muttering something. Two men in denim jackets were flinging themselves against the rear of the car. "Now!" one shouted, and I felt the thud of their bodies. The wheels spun. "Dunderheads," said Jake, shutting off the ignition. "If those two would get together, for once . . ."

"What's going on?" I asked him.

He gave me a slit-eyed look and got out of the car. "What we need is that there tractor," I heard him telling the men. "All you got to do is bring it up behind and give her a shove."

"Tractor? What tractor?" one man asked. "You talking about that yonder? Why, she's just a little old twelve-horse thing my wife uses for the kitchen garden. You think we're going to push you out with that? And there's no way of getting in behind you; this bank is rising up too steep to your rear."

"Pull her from ahead then, I don't care."

"Pull her neither, you're looking at a toy. That thing don't even tote manure good."

"Look," said Jake, "I got twenty dollars says you can do it if you work it right."

Through the rear window, I saw him dealing out money to the man in the red plaid cap. Little puffs of mist were coming from their mouths. "In *ones?*" the man said.

"Money's money."

"Well, I reckon we could give her a try. Come on, Cade."

He and Cade walked off across the field. Jake got back in the car, bringing cool air with him, and I shivered and folded my arms across my chest. I felt dislocated; I had somehow lost a whole night. "Where are we, anyway?" I asked.

"If you would take a look out the window, you'd see we're in a wheat field."

"I mean, how'd we get here?"

"Guess I fell asleep at the wheel," Jake said. He started rubbing his chin, which was bristly by now. "Fact is, I must have," he said, "but it don't make sense. I am known for not sleeping, see. I just don't need sleep like most people do. At a party or something I can stay up all night and be on about my business in the morning same as usual, stay up the next night too if I've a mind to. Gets lonesome, sometimes. Everyone sacked out and me awake. But there you are: I was just driving along not thinking a thing and next I know I'm in a wheat field. Middle of the night, no one about; and you were just dead to the world. All there was to do was go on back to sleep. Had me some wait this morning too till I seen these fellows come stomping through the oats."

"Wheat," I said, though to be honest I couldn't tell one from the other. I squinted out the window at the yellow weeds.

I saw the man in the cap driving toward us on a little green tractor, while Cade walked beside him swinging a few loops of rope. "Watch, now," Jake said. "That baby'll get us out quick as a cricket, wait and see. I been in lots worse spots than this." He rolled down his window and shouted, "Hitch her up, guys, then take her nice and easy. Don't pull too sudden."

The men ignored him and went about their work. Jake didn't know how to deal with them, I thought. I was ashamed to be found in his company and I scrunched down lower in my seat, so I didn't see them hitching us. I felt it, though. I had been in this car so long it was like a second skin to me. I felt, or thought I felt, their knotty hands fumbling at the bumper, running a raspy rope through and tying it. Then Cade came up to Jake's window. "You going to let the lady out?" he asked.

Jake thought a minute. "Naw," he said.

"Give you a mite less weight."

"Her door is busted," said Jake. "Never mind all that." He turned the key in the ignition. Cade stepped back, and the tractor increased the sound of its motor to a high, complaining hum. I felt the rope go tight. Our tires whizzed. We moved ahead a foot or two. Then we jerked and I heard a *ping!* and the car came to a halt. I sat up straighter and looked out the window, just in time to see our front bumper go trundling across the field. "Jesus," Jake said.

The tractor stopped and the driver slid off. The two men returned, scratching their heads. Jake got out of the car and went to join them. Now all three were scratching their heads, and frowning at where the bumper used to be. "This here is a genuine, nineteen fifty-three Woolworth's," said Jake. The men nodded, as if making notes. "And look at these tires, slick as a garden hose." He kicked one. I felt the jarring. There was a long, solemn silence.

Then: "Well, I tell you," the tractor driver said. "I feel real bad about your bumper."

"Wasn't *your* fault," said Jake.

"But I'm wondering could we push her now. See, she's out of that slant some, you notice? Nose ain't pointed to the ground so. Maybe the lady could take the wheel and then us three could push."

Jake came back and stuck his head in the window. "I don't drive," I said before he could ask.

"You know where the gas pedal is."

"No, I don't, and what's worse I have no notion where the brake is."

"Sure you do," Jake said. He got in and started the engine again. He pointed to the floor: gas, brake. "But lay off of the brake," he told me, "till you get to that there road up ahead. See it? You can't see it. Little farm road. Gravel. We're going to push her over there instead of the highway. There's no *way* she can climb that bank to the highway. Okay, slide over."

He got out. I slid over. "She ain't too much of a driver," Jake said, and the men grunted. I saw now that they got along fine; the three of them stood shoulder to shoulder, resigned, watching my white-knuckled hands on the wheel. Cade said, "Don't be scared, lady, just give it to her slow."

"All right," I said.

"Won't do to have her spin herself a rut."

"Of course not."

They walked off to the rear, out of sight. I felt them settling behind the car. "Okay," Jake called, "got your foot on the brake?"

I nodded.

"What?"

"*Yes.*"

"Shift to Drive. D."

I shifted. The motor changed its tone.

"Now the gas."

I pressed the gas pedal. The men threw their weight

against the fender. The wheels whined and spun. Then slowly, bumpily, the car inched ahead. It picked up speed. It got free of the men, it bounded over ruts and boulders, scratching its way through the weeds, leaving a flattened yellow ribbon behind. I looked in the mirror and saw the ribbon and the men running down it, waving and shouting. But I had forgotten to look in front of me and found, too late, the little gravel road springing up and fading away again. I panicked and pressed the gas pedal harder. Then I pulled back on the steering wheel. Then I shifted through the gears till I hit on one that screeched the tires, stopped the car dead, and flung me into the windshield. When Jake came up, I saw him through a veil of colored ovals swimming around in black air. I had some sort of extra surface on the center of my forehead. "See?" Jake told me. "Who says you can't drive?" He climbed into the car, while I floated over to the passenger side. Then he restarted the engine and backed onto the gravel road. He waved to his friends, who were ambling toward us across the field. They waved back. We set off toward the highway.

"I could eat a horse," said Jake. "Couldn't you?"

But I was shaking too much to answer.

We had breakfast at a Sunoco station: a bag of bacon rinds and two Yoo-Hoos from a vending machine. I used the restroom, and stood a while staring into the mirror on the paper towel dispenser. I felt I had to gather myself together again. My own eyes stared back at me, surprisingly dark. (I had half expected to find them bleached as gray as Jake's.) My face appeared pinched and confused. It was a relief to grab up my purse and go back to the car.

This was piney country we were passing through, dotted with farms and new, raw-looking cinderblock supermarkets. Periodically we would land behind some truck or tractor, with no possible way of passing, and then Jake would start muttering. "Pokey old fool! Hayseed. Dimwit. Good mind to ram him in the tail."

"Well, I don't understand," I said. "Now surely Maryland is not the only state with divided highways. Is this all the road they have here?"

"All the road *I'm* taking," said Jake. "You know durn well no cop is going to bother with it."

I thought he had too much faith, but it's true we weren't seeing any patrol cars. Just crumpled Chevies, Fords, and those everlasting trucks. When Jake's temper gave out, every fifteen minutes or so, he would pull up at one of the supermarkets and get us something to eat. Fritos. Oreos. I chewed in time to a whole chorus of TV commercials singing inside my head. Meanwhile Jake would gun his motor and push on, arriving finally behind the selfsame truck that had held him back in the first place. And always on a hill or curve, or with oncoming cars in the other lane. He cursed. I went on chewing. I am gifted with the ability of giving up, and all I had to do was pretend we were on some great, smooth, slow conveyor belt, coasting through the billboarded countryside two and a half feet behind a truckful of lawnmowers.

For lunch we stopped at a diner on the outskirts of a city. "But we've eaten all morning," I said. "I'm not hungry."

"That don't make no difference. Point is, I rest."

There were factories and auto graveyards everywhere we looked, and the diner sat on the tiniest concrete apron as if something had been nibbling away at it. Inside, it was full of brushed aluminum and gold-flecked, aging vinyl. The only other customer was a teenager eating a hot dog. The waitress was a stern-faced, churchy woman in tin-rimmed glasses. She curled her mouth downward while taking Jake's order: everything grilled, greased, salted. (I was beginning to know his

eating tastes, by now.) "Just coffee for me," I said. The waitress sniffed and stalked off.

When she was gone, I reached over to the stool beside me
and picked up a newspaper. Used, badly refolded, but all of it
was there. "Want the funnies?" I asked Jake. He looked disgusted. I shrugged. I scanned the first page, then the second.
Primaries, cost of living, labor contracts . . . not a word about
Jake or me. We'd dropped out of people's minds, might not
even have existed. They'd moved on to more important con-
cerns. I was stunned. Jake wasn't, though. When I lowered the
paper, he didn't even glance up. He was too busy filling his
pockets with Domino sugar packs.

"We're not in here," I told him.

"Huh?" he said. He looked around the diner.

"In the paper. Not in the paper."

"So?"

The waitress brought our order. I sat staring into my
coffee, not touching it. Jake hitched up his jacket sleeves and
reached across me for the salt. "How much cash you got?" he
asked me.

"Cash?"

"I need to find out."

"It's none of your business," I said.

"I know you got some, I saw it in your billfold."

"That's my own private money," I said.

Ordinarily I don't give a hoot about money, never have;
but this was different. I was on my own and forgotten, deserted
by everyone who should have been hunting me, and here was
this stranger trying to take my last means of support. Also, my
feelings were hurt. I'd enjoyed having somebody buy me
things, to tell the truth. I said, "You might show a little consid-
eration."

"Look. Lady," said Jake. "Charlotte. This trip ain't
cheap, for the gas alone. I'm running short. Now as a rule I

would no more take from a individual person than *fly*, but in this case I have got to ask you for your billfold."

I pretended not to hear him.

"Let's just say it's a loan," he said.

"I don't want to loan it."

"I'm begging you. I got to have it. What you think, those puny dollar bills will last forever?"

The waitress glanced over her shoulder at us. Light flashed off her spectacles.

"You're killing me," Jake said. "Just sitting here killing me."

His voice was low but cracking around the edges, and I could tell he was about to throw a scene. I hate scenes. I took the billfold out of my purse and slapped it down on the counter.

"Ah," said Jake.

"Seven measly dollars," I said. "I certainly hope you're satisfied."

"Word of honor I'll pay it back, Charlotte. Cross my heart."

"I bet," I said.

I rested my chin on my fist. Brooded over my coffee, blinking in the steam. Looked around for sugar, but the metal rack was empty. I could have cried. "There's no *sugar!*" I said.

"Well, there," said Jake, and fished up a pack from his pocket. He opened it and poured it in for me. I sat back and watched. Then he added cream, and stirred it with a plastic spoon. "Drink it," he told me.

I felt comforted. All I had to do was lift the cup, which was warm and heavy and solid. Everything else had been seen to. I was so well taken care of.

8

After Saul and I were engaged, my mother made some adjustments in her thinking. I suppose she imagined ways of keeping us with her forever, somehow. She acted friendlier toward him. She grew more animated and had to be taken to look at wedding gowns. Her heart's desire was a real church wedding, she said. Saul said that would be fine. Not a one of us *belonged* to a church, but why point that out? I just drifted along. There was a satisfying heaviness in my hands and feet that made me move unusually slowly. Though sometimes I'd sit up with my heart pounding; I'd wonder: Am I really going to do this? Go on through with this? What can I be thinking of? But then I'd make my mind go blank. My muscles would loosen, and the heaviness would swim back over me.

Taking pictures now, I froze so long behind the camera that you might ask who was getting preserved here: my customers or me. Sitting with Saul in the evenings, I sheltered under his arm and listened to him plot our lives. He wanted six children. I assumed I couldn't have any (having inherited, in some illogical way, my mother's non-pregnancy and untrue baby) but I nodded, even so. I imagined six dark, unreadable little boys with Saul's straight nose, hanging onto my skirts. I imagined myself suddenly as colorful, rich, and warm as Alberta, my narrow, parched life opening like a flower. All I had to do was give myself up. Easy. I let him lead me. I agreed to everything. It was such a pleasure that I felt soothed and sleepy, like a cat in sunshine.

Mama said there was nothing fit to wear in the bridal shops, and she started making my dress at home. White satin, high-necked, with buttoned sleeves. Evidently she wasn't planning on a summer wedding. It was almost June by then. Saul's money was running low. He still hadn't found what he wanted to do. All *I* wanted to do was sleep with Saul, but that went against his convictions. He had tomcatted long enough, he said, and was looking now for a home, a family, a steady way of life. And he wouldn't marry me till he found a job; everything had to be perfect. I myself would rather have been married immediately, but I didn't argue. In this new mood of mine, I only smiled. My hands and feet grew heavier every day; my eyes took on the pearly glow of someone in a trance.

Then Saul caught a bus to Colorado. He went to see an old Army buddy; they were going to talk about a partnership in something. Maybe some kind of a shop where they could work with their hands. I should keep my fingers crossed, he told me. He was aiming for a June wedding.

That was terrible, that time he was gone. I felt I'd just waked from some long, pillowy dream and taken a look at where I was: still friendless, sallow, peculiar, living alone with my mother, surrounded by monstrous potted plants taller and older than I was. Rubber trees and Chinese palms that hadn't put out a new leaf since I was born. Mildewed sets of the classics locked in glass-fronted bookshelves, dusty candy in pedestaled dishes. And Mama newly anxious over this trip to Colorado, fretting and mumbling and letting my wedding gown fall apart on the dress form in the dining room. Would I really consider going so far? she asked. Was I taking her along?

I would consider going anywhere, anywhere at all. And I wasn't taking Mama.

I moved to Saul's room. (Mama was shocked.) Saul had a lot of clutter too but at least there was life in his clutter. All his Army things smelled salty and wild. What little he had saved from Alberta's house—a green metal toolchest and two hunting rifles—had a self-contained look. I stared for hours at a group photo of Edwin, the four boys, and a birthday cake, with a clipped-out square at the center of the picture. I slept in his hard sleigh bed, I wrapped up in his terrycloth bathrobe, and occasionally I slipped my feet into a pair of his shoes. But still I couldn't seem to step inside his life. Clomping along, trailing an extra six inches of terrycloth sleeve, I would wade to the window and lean out to memorize his view: Alberta's house, with the panes gone now and the roof ripped off. I opened his closet just to breathe in his clothing, and once even heaved a rifle onto my shoulder and laid my cheek against the oiled wood of the handle. Squinting along the bluish barrel, resting my finger on a trigger no more complicated than a camera button, I could easily imagine shooting someone. It's the completed action: once you've taken aim, how can you resist the pull to follow through?

Saul was gone ten days, but came back with nothing settled. He hadn't liked his friend as much as he'd remembered. He didn't know; they just hadn't hit it off, somehow. He would rather keep on looking. Rather wait for whatever felt right.

That evening I put on a floating nightgown, and listened for Mama's door to close. Then I went skimming through the dark to his salty-smelling room, to his hard sleigh bed, to his window full of moonlight and Alberta's tottering house.

In the morning, he said maybe we should go on ahead with the wedding.

It wasn't a June wedding after all. We got married in July. That's because we had to go to Holy Basis Church for a month before the preacher there would marry us. Holy Basis was this total-dunking, hellfire place where Edwin Emory used to be a deacon, and Saul had conceived the notion that he'd like to hold the wedding there. Well, *I* had no church, wasn't religious in any way at all; and Mama'd quit Clarion Methodist some twenty years back over an insult she'd overheard. So for four Sundays straight we went to Holy Basis, with its fake-brick tarpaper and its smoky wooden ceiling, hymn numbers scrawled on a slate up front and Reverend Davitt just droning and intoning—a beak-nosed man in black who clung to the pulpit for dear life. Saul and I sat very near the front. (We wanted to be counted.) We were close enough to see the tears of the people on the mourners' bench, and the fluttering of their eyelids when they raised their faces in prayer. "What are they mourning?" I asked Saul once when we were walking home, and he said, "Their sins."

"Why not call it the rejoicing bench," I said, "if that's where they go to be reborn."

"Yes, but first they have to repent their past ways."

"You certainly know a lot about it," I said.

"Oh, *I've* been on the mourners' bench."

"You have?"

"Of course."

"You've been . . . saved?"

"Saved and repented and dunked in Clarion Lake," he told me. "Before I joined the Army."

I couldn't get over it. I walked the rest of the way home in

total silence. I just never had realized how very different from
me he really was.

Mama wouldn't finish my gown. I suspected her of pulling out
seams every night. The day before my wedding I said, "Look
here, Mama, it's all the same to me if I get married in my black
lace slip. I mean, not having that dress won't stop the wedding." So she got down to work then, sewed all afternoon and
then had me stand on the dining room table while she pinned
up the hem. I revolved slowly, like a bride on a music box.
Mama talked on and on about Grandma Debney's china,
which I was to have, but I didn't really listen. Some little string
of sadness kept pulling at my mind.

After that we went to the studio and I set up the camera.
Then Mama took a picture of Saul and me. We stood very
straight, like an old-fashioned couple, while Mama said,
"Where is it? What do I pull out? How do I go about this?"
Then I took a picture of Saul with his arm around Mama. "Oh
no, please, I'm not photogenic," she said, but he said, "Mother
Ames, you're a member of my family now, and I need your
portrait for my family album."

"It's sweet of you to be so nice to her," I told him later.

"Nice? Who's being nice?" he said. "I meant it."

And I could see that he did.

It was a small wedding. No bridesmaids, no best man.
(Saul had wanted one of his brothers, but none could make it.)
He wouldn't let me invite Alberta, but my uncle's family came
and so did a few Holy Basis members who'd seen the announcement in the bulletin. Later we drove to Ocean City in
my father's old pickup, which Saul had repaired and repainted.
We hardly swam at all, though. Saul spent his days pacing by
the edge of the water while I lay flat on the sand, recuperating
from the years of loneliness, warming and glowing and deepen-
ing all week long.

I remember the date: July 14, 1960. A Thursday. We'd been back from Ocean City five days. I was in the studio, cropping an enlargement. Mama was knitting on the couch. Saul walked in the door with an envelope. He said he would like to talk to me a minute.

"Why, surely," I said.

Already I felt uneasy.

I followed him up the stairs to his room. Our room, it was now. I sat on the sleigh bed. He started walking back and forth, slapping the envelope against one palm. "Listen to what I'm going to say," he told me. I swallowed and sat up straighter.

"All along," he said, "I've been wondering why things are working out like this. Finding *you*, I mean, just at this point in my life. Oh, I did plan that when I got out of the Army I'd like a wife and home. But first I had to make a living. So that day when you opened the door, and wore that faded soft sweater— well, why *now?* I wanted to know. When I've got no means to support her and nothing steady to offer. Couldn't this have waited? Then I tried believing I should let you pass by, but it wasn't possible. Well, now I have the answer, Charlotte. I know what it's all about."

He stopped pacing, and turned and smiled down at me. I felt more puzzled than ever. I said, "You do?"

"Charlotte," Saul said, "I've been called to preach."

"Been—*what?*"

"Don't you see? That's what it was. If I hadn't met you I wouldn't have gone back to Holy Basis Church, I might never have known what I was supposed to do. Now it's plain."

Well. I was so stunned I couldn't even take in air. I mean I just wasn't prepared for this, nothing that had happened up till now had given me the faintest inkling. I said, "But . . . but, Saul . . ."

"Let me tell you how it came about," he said. "Remember

that Sunday I helped pack the hymnbooks? I carried a box to the basement. I passed the preschool room where I used to stay when I was a kid. Had its same old blue linoleum and those pipes they were always telling us not to swing on. Then I heard this song: me and my three brothers singing 'Love Lifted Me.' I swear it. Do you believe me? Our identical voices, I couldn't mistake them. I just stood there with my mouth open. I even heard that lisp of Julian's he lost when his second teeth came in. We sang two lines and got fainter on the third and then drifted off, still singing."

"Well, wait," I said. "The four of you *together?* In the preschool room? Surely that never happened, there's too much difference in your ages."

"This is not all that logical," Saul told me.

"No, it certainly isn't," I said.

"Reverend Davitt felt it was an experience of a religious nature."

I didn't like the way he phrased it. Certain parts of him suddenly began to seem preacherly—even his bone structure, the echo in his voice, the tranquil gaze that could also be viewed as complacent, I saw now. Why hadn't I noticed before? I'd been too busy gathering other messages, that's why. I hadn't even had a warning twinge.

Still, I held out. "But listen, Saul," I said. "Maybe it was leftover sound waves or something, have you thought of that?"

"He felt it might be a call to preach. We had several talks about it," Saul said.

I watched him open the envelope, with long brown fingers that could easily be pictured turning the pages of a Bible. Although I didn't believe in God, I could almost change my mind now and imagine one, for who else would play such a joke on me? The only place more closed-in than this house was a church. The only person odder than my mother was a hellfire preacher. I nearly laughed. I took a mild, amused interest in the sheet of paper he pulled from the envelope.

"This is what came in the mail today. I didn't want to tell you till I got it," he said. "A letter of acceptance from the Hamden Bible College."

"Bible College," I said.

"Oh, I know it takes money. The Army won't pay for a school that's not accredited—pure prejudice. But look at the advantages: Hamden's just a two-year school, and half an hour away. We can live right here with your mother! I'll reopen Dad's radio shop and that'll pay the tuition. For I know I'm meant to stay in Clarion, Charlotte. This all came to me; it's what I have to do. Don't you see?"

All I saw was the view from his window: a cross-section of Alberta's house with flowered wallpaper, copper pipes writhing toward the sky, and a medicine cabinet wide open and empty. It was very clear: they were tearing down the rest of the world completely. They were leaving no place standing but my mother's. They were keeping me here forever, all the long, slow days of my life.

9

We drove through an endless afternoon, passing scenery that appeared to have wilted. Crumbling sheds and unpainted houses, bony cattle drooping over fences. "Whereabouts *is* this?" I finally asked.

"Georgia," said Jake.

"Georgia!"

I sat up straighter and looked around me. I had never imagined finding myself in Georgia. But still there wasn't much to see. "Well," I said, "I tell you what. I think I'll go in the back and take a nap."

"No," said Jake.

"Why not?"

"I ain't going to have you slipping away from me. You would open that door and slip right away."

"Well, for goodness sake," I said. I felt insulted. "Why

would I do that? All I want is a little sleep. *Lock* the door, if you like."

"No way of doing that."

"Get another chain from somewhere."

"What, and lock myself in too?"

"You could keep a key. Find one of those—"

"Lay off of me, Charlotte."

I was quiet for a while. I studied snuff adds. Then I said, "You really ought to get over this thing about locks, you know."

"Lay off, I said."

I looked for a radio, but there wasn't one. I opened the glove compartment to check the insides: road maps, a flashlight, cigarettes, boring things like that. I slammed it shut. I said, "Jake."

"Hmm."

"Where're we going, anyway?"

He glanced over at me. "*Now* you ask," he said. "I was starting to think you had something missing."

"Missing?"

"Some nut or bolt or something. Not to wonder before now where we was headed."

"Well, I had no idea we were heading to some *point*," I said.

"You thought I was doing all this driving for the fun of it."

"Where are we going, Jake?"

"Perth, Florida," said Jake.

"Perth?"

"That's where Oliver lives. My friend from training school."

"Oh, Oliver."

"See, his mother moved him to Florida to get him out of trouble. Opened her a motel there. A widow lady. She never did think much of me, moved Oliver clean away from me. Now we're going to look him up, with a stop-off first in Linex, Georgia."

"What's in Linex?" I asked.

He started rummaging through his pockets. First his jacket, then his trouser pockets. Finally he came up with a piece of notebook paper. He held it out to me. "What's this?" I said.

"Read it."

I unfolded it and smoothed the creases. The writing had been done with a hard lead pencil—one of those that leaves the other side of the paper embossed. All the i's were dotted with fat hearts.

> Dear Jake,
>
> Honey please come get me soon! Its like a prison here. I had been expecting you long ago. Didn't you get my letter? I called your home but your mother said she didn't know where you were. Do you want for your son to be born in a prison?
>
> Love and xxx!
>
> Mindy

I read it twice. Then I looked at Jake.

"Now, that I couldn't abide," said Jake.

"What's that?"

"My son to be born in a prison."

"What's she in prison for?"

"She ain't in prison, she's in a home for unwed mothers."

"Oh, I see," I said.

"Her mother is this devil, real devil. Sent her off to this home her church runs, never let me hear word one about it till Mindy was packed and gone. Mindy is a minor," he said.

I was slow: I thought he meant she worked in a mine. I saw a rich, black, underground world opening at my feet, where everyone was in some deep and dramatic trouble. I felt too pale for all this and I drew away, folding the letter primly. "She's too young to have a say," said Jake, but even after I understood I kept picturing her in someplace dark. "She's not but seventeen years old. But in my estimation they should have let her decide for herself, and me as well. I mean me and her been going together for three whole years, off and on."

"Well, wait," I said. "Three *years?*"

"She was fourteen," said Jake, "but right well developed."

"I never heard of such a thing."

"Okay, Miss Priss, but it wasn't *my* fault. She just set her heart on me. She just fixed on me and wouldn't let go. See, she lived down the road from me and my mom a ways, Route Four outside of Clarion on the Pimsah River. Know the place? We'd been half acquainted for years, but not to speak to. Then her and her family come to watch this derby, and it just so happened I was driving in it and won. I guess in her eyes that must have made me some kind of a hero. After that she commenced to following me around, calling me on the telephone and bringing me picnic lunches and beers she had stole from her daddy. Her daddy was Darnell Callender, owns a feed store, you may have heard of him. Always wears a Panama hat. Well, at first I thought she was too young and besides I didn't like her all that much but I couldn't seem to shake her. She was forever hanging around and didn't take offense when I sent her away but went off smiling, made me feel bad. Just a *little* gal, you know? It was summer and she wore these sandals like threads, real breakable-looking. Finally it just seemed like I might as well go on out with her.

"But we weren't never what you would call steady," he said. "I would oftentimes be seeing other girls and all. I would ask myself, 'Now how did I get mixed up with this Mindy anyhow, what's the point of it?' She talked too much, and not about nothing I cared for. Sometimes it seemed like she was so boring I just couldn't find enough air to breathe when I was around her. But sometimes, why, she'd say something to me direct that showed me how she watched me, how she *saw* me, you know? And I would think, This person is bound to have something to do with me. I mean it ain't love, but what is it? Worse than love, harder to break. Like we had to wear each other through, work something out, I don't know. I swear, she like to drove me crazy. I'd say to myself, I'd say, 'Why, she ain't nothing but a hindrance. I don't need to put up with this.' Then we would part. But like always, she'd go smiling. And then later she'd keep coming around and *coming* around, and somehow I'd end up in the same old situation again. You understand?"

I nodded. I could see it all happening but had not, up till now, imagined that it could happen to Jake.

"Then last fall, she calls me on the phone. Tells me she's expecting. A fluke: we were having one of our partings. I hadn't been near her since August. Ordinarily I would try not to tamper with her anyway, but you know how it is sometimes. And I *will* say she had some part in it. A big part. I mean she would just . . . so there I was. What could I do? It had come up so sudden. Well, if she had wrote a letter maybe, give me time to think. But no, she has to telephone. 'Going to have a baby, Jake.' Happy as a queen. Says to me, 'I think we better get married.'

"I was surprised, that's all. If I'd have thought I would have said, 'Now cool down, Mindy, we'll figure some other way of doing this.' But I was surprised. I said, 'Are you out of your flipping mind? Have you lost your marbles? Do you really believe I would get married, go that whole soft-living route?' I said. 'Let alone marry *you*.' Then I hung up. I was fit to be tied, I was as mad as I could get. But I know I should have handled it better than what I did."

"You were just startled," I told him.

I didn't mean to take his side like that. But I was touched by the tense, despairing way his hands were gripping the steering wheel. His bitten fingernails pained me. "I would have said the same thing," I told him.

"Well," said Jake. "Week or two passes, month or two passes, I get to thinking. I hadn't seen her in all that time and was starting to notice she was missing. Pictures would pop into my mind. Them perky little bandannas she wore. Way she was always after me to do my magic tricks, and clapped when I was through. Like she was really just a child, you know? Always humming, skipping, swinging my hand when we walked . . . then I got to wondering how she would stay with her mother, devil of a mother; they hadn't never hit it off too good. So I thought, Well, least I could do is be of some help to her in this. It's true I never asked for it but I would hate to feel to blame in any way.' I mean, I'm not a *bad* man. Am I?"

"Of course not," I said.

"I called her house. Her mother says, 'Too late, Jake Simms.' Took me three full weeks to track her down. I had to ask her Cousin Cobb. Then I wrote her a letter. I wanted to know if she was okay and needed anything sent. And she wrote back, 'What I need is *out*. Please come and get me.'

"Well, I could do that. Question was, where to put her after I got her. If she was just older she might have some married girlfriend or such that she could stay with, but I don't guess she does and so I thought I would take her on to Florida and look up O.J. Him and me have always kept in touch, you see. He sends me these Christmas cards. And I like to think about him a lot and him reading his books no matter who locks him up.

"I figured Mindy could stay in Florida till the baby comes and then we'd give it out for adoption. I don't think Mindy would make such a hot mother anyhow. Then she could go on back but I might stay in Florida. They have very fine derbies in

Florida. Maybe Oliver and me could room together, like the old days.

"But to get to Florida first you got to have the money, right? And I didn't have none. I was unemployed; this body shop where I sometimes work had fired me unfairly. Derby season was over and I hadn't done so good there anyhow. I was having to hang around the house, just rising late and hunting in the icebox and watching TV. Soap operas. Game shows. People winning a thousand tins of cat food or a heart-shaped bed, and all you got to fill your mind is, 'Wonder where they'll find the sheets to fit it?' Stuff like that. I'd always been the kind to spend what I got when I got it and now I didn't have no savings, couldn't even help on the groceries. It was sorry times.

"And friends? Used to be you could borrow from your friends, but I don't know, lately it seems to me like all my friends have gone and married on me. Some of my coolest, finest friends have up and married. I can't get over it. Leaving me right lonesome, and you know how little cash a married man would have free to lend. Seems like they're always saving up for a automatic grill and such. There wasn't no hope there.

"Well, I tell you what I did. I went to my brother-in-law, Marvel Hodge. He runs Marvelous Chevrolet. I'm sure you've heard of him. Anytime anything gets to happening on the 'Late Show' they break it off and here comes Marvel, wide-faced man with scalloped hair, grinning and slapping a fender. Why my sister married him I'll never know. I can't stand the sight of him, myself.

"But I went to him. I drove in to see him in Mom's old Ford. (Has he ever given her a free Chevy? No. No, nor not even a used one.) I found him out on the lot, kidding around with some customers in this ho-ho way he has. I said, 'Marvel, like to talk with you a minute.'

"He says, 'Go ahead, Jake.'

"Right in front of all those people, that's the kind of man he is.

"I said, 'Marvel, even though you're supposed to be some relation to me I'm not such a fool as to ask you for a gift or a loan. I do need money bad but I ain't going to ask that. All I want is a job, fair and square. Just to tide me over,' I said. 'You know full well I'm smarter when it comes to cars than any three men you got. How about it.'

"Know what he did? He started laughing. Starts laughing and shaking his head. Right in front of these customers, whole family: man and wife and two little girls and some kind of uncle or something. 'Boy,' he says, 'now I've heard everything. A *job*, you say. Give Jake Simms a job, that never was out of trouble since the very first day he was born. Why, I'd have to be a total fool.'

"I kept my temper, I will say that. I said, 'Marvel, I may have done one or two hasty things in my younger days but you got no right to hold that over my head. I'm a grown man now,' I said, 'and never get in no more trouble than taking a extra drink or two on a Saturday night. I'd like you to reconsider your words, if you please.'

" 'Grown?' says Marvel. 'Grown? I doubt I'll live to see the day,' he says. 'Go on, boy, leave me to these good people here.'

"Well, I *still* kept my temper. Walked back to my Ford, real quiet—felt like I was about to burst but I didn't say a word. Climbed in, started the engine, fixed the rear-view mirror a little straighter so as I could prepare to back out. But I didn't back out, I went forward. Well, I don't know how it happened. I mean I did intend to do it but I didn't *know* I was going to do it. I just raced full forward into the car lot, and Marvel sprang left and his customers sprang right. Hit a new Bel Air, buckled in the whole right side. Backed off and hit a Vega. Set on down the row of them, crushing everything I come upon. Fenders was crumpled like paper, bumpers curled, doors falling off— and this crunchy feeling every time I hit and everybody scream-ing and dancing. Of course my own car got dented some too, but not what you would expect. I believe I could've drove her on home, in fact, till I took this notion to hit a Monza head-on. See, in a derby you just don't hit head-on. The rules don't allow it. So I got this urge. I hit head-on and the two of them cars went up like the Fourth of July, and I rolled out as quick as I could and was picked off the concrete by three cops."

I laughed. Jake glanced over at me as if he'd forgotten I was there.

"Later they all tore into me," he said, "even Mom, asking how come I hadn't held my temper. But I kept telling them I *did* hold my temper, for I could have mowed down Marvel and his customers as well but I restrained myself.

"I restrained myself in the jail too and tried hard not to escape. I had determined to be a reasonable man, you see. I just sat tight and waited for my trial. No one that knew me would bail me out, and my mom didn't have no cash. I had to stay in. It wasn't easy. I had these funny kinds of sweats at times and hives come up over nine-tenths of my body, but still I held back from escaping.

"Now, this lawyer they got me said I ought to plead guilty. He said there wasn't no question about it. I said I would be telling a falsehood, if I did that. I said I had been forced to wreck that place, had no choice in the matter whatsoever; Marvel Hodge just drove me to it. 'Call that guilty?' I said. 'No sir, I'm pleading innocent.' We argued back and forth some over that. And time was passing. Understand that every day was just stretching me one more inch beyond the breaking point. But I held tight, I held tight.

"Day before the trial, Mom brought me this letter. She was my only visitor, see. Sally, my sister, she wasn't speaking to me. And naturally Marvel didn't come. If he had of I'd have killed him. Broke out of my cell and killed him.

"Mom brought this letter from Mindy, one I showed you. Addressed to the house. Evidently Mindy hadn't heard about my trouble. Her mother either didn't know or hadn't passed the news on, one; though I can't imagine her missing the chance. Anyhow, here's this letter, asking if I wanted for my son to be born in a prison. That tore me up, I tell you. Seems like I just went wild. How come this world has so many ways of tying a person down? Now there is no *way* I would sit by and let that happen.

"Next morning they come to take me to the courthouse and on Harp Street I slipped loose, with this one guard's gun handy in my pocket. Nothing to it. They watch you less careful on the way to a trial; they know you're thinking far ahead, got some hope of being cleared. Except me. I didn't have no hope at all. I was like, barred, boxed in. Everybody carried such a set notion of me. I knew the only hope I had was to get away.

"How did I go so wrong? I thought I would clear a thousand at least, hitting that bank. Thought I would be free then and unencumbered. But here we are. Seems like everything got bungled. Every step was stupid, every inch of the way. Every move I made was worse than the one before."

"You were just unlucky," I told him. "Never mind."

"When you think," said Jake, "that I set all this in motion just to show I ain't a bad man, don't it make you want to laugh?"

Late in the afternoon we arrived in Linex, which seemed to be one very wide, empty street. We stopped in front of a grocery store to use the phone booth. "Now the name of this place is the Dorothea Whitman Home," said Jake. He was leafing through the directory, which was no thicker than a pamphlet. His stubby finger slid down the columns. He had kept the door open and I looked past his shoulder to see, of all things, butterflies, spangling the yellow air. We truly had traveled; we'd left that cold false Maryland spring behind and found a real one. "Look!" I said, and Jake spun toward the door. "Butterflies," I told him.

"Will you let me get on with this?"

I wasn't wearing my raincoat any more and he had un-
zipped his jacket. We were showing whole new layers: identical
white shirts. Glassed in the way we were, under the last of the
sunlight, we both had a thin shine of sweat like plants in a
greenhouse. "In Clarion, it may be snowing," I said.

"Not likely," said Jake. His finger had found its mark and
stopped. "Dorothea Whitman Home," he said. "I'll dial, you
talk."

"How come *I* have to talk?"

"You don't think they'd let a man through."

"I can't imagine why not."

"Well, I ain't taking no chances. Ask for Mindy Callender, say it's her aunt or something."

He dropped in a dime and dialed. I pressed the receiver to
my ear. A woman answered: "Whitman Home."

"Mindy Callender, please," I said.

"One moment."

Something in the lines turned off and on. There was a
pause and then a thin voice said, "Hello?"

"Hello. Mindy?"

"Who's this?"

I handed the receiver to Jake. "Hey there," he said. He
grinned. "Yeah, yeah, it's me. I'm here. No, that was just—
well, I'm fine. How're you?"

He listened a long time. His face grew serious again.
"Sorry to hear that," he said. "Really? Well, I'm sorry to . . .
look here, Mindy, I need to know something. Has anybody
been asking for me? Asking if you knew my whereabouts? You
sure, now. *No* I'm not in no trouble, quit that. Just tell me
where to come for you."

I pressed my back against the glass of the booth, trying to
get more room. I watched Jake's fingers tap the directory and
then grow still. "Why not?" he said. "It ain't even dark yet.

Look, now, Mindy, we're in sort of a hurry here, we . . . how's that? Naw. What would I be doing with a ladder?"

He listened a while longer. "Yeah, well," he said. "First left after the . . . sure. *Sure* I got it, I ain't that stupid. Okay. Bye."

He hung up and dug his fingers into his hair. "Shoot," he said.

"What's the matter?"

"First she says she can't get free today, wants me to come at midnight instead and fetch her down a ladder. A ladder! I tell you, sometimes that Mindy is so . . . and when I say no, she says then maybe she'll meet me at six tomorrow morning. Maybe, maybe not. What is she playing at now?"

"I would think a ladder would be sort of . . . risky," I said.

"You don't know Mindy, that's just the kind of thing she admires," he said. "I'm surprised she don't want me charging up on a horse."

We left the booth and went into the grocery store. Jake chose a Gillette, a can of lather, a giant bottle of Coke, and a bag of Doritos. I saw a freezer full of orange juice and developed a craving for some, but he said it would be too much trouble to mix. He was very short-tempered, I thought. He cruised the aisles, muttering to himself, hurrying me along whenever I slowed down. "Come on, come on, we ain't got all night."

"The way I see it, all night's just what we do have," I said.

"This is not the time to start acting smart," he told me.

After we'd finished in the grocery store we drove on through Linex, which had turned a silvery color now that the sun was down. We traveled so far I wondered if we were going for good, giving up on Mindy. I thought that would be fine. (Even leaving someone *else's* loved one could fill me with a

kind of wicked joy.) But then Jake slowed the car and peered
at the woods to his right. He said, "This here will have to do, I
guess." A brown wooden sign spelled out TUNSAQUIT KAMP-
GROUNDS in chiseled letters. We turned onto a dirt road and
bounced along, passing an empty bulletin board, a Johnny-
on-the-Spot, and several trashcans. Finally the road ended.
Jake stopped the car and slumped back. "Well," I said.

"Yeah, well," he said.

He rolled down the window. This deep in the woods it was
already twilight, and a mushroom-smelling chill hit us like a
faceful of damp leaves. He rolled the window up again. "I
thought at least they'd have picnic tables," he said.

"Maybe we could try further on."

"Nah."

I pulled my raincoat around me but Jake just sat there,
drumming his fingers on the steering wheel. Finally I reached
into the grocery bag and opened the Doritos. "Have some," I
said. He shook his head. I took a handful myself and ate them
one by one. "They're good," I told him. "Try and see."

"I ain't hungry."

"If we just had that orange juice they'd be perfect."

"Now, how'd we mix orange juice way off here in the
woods? Besides, I had to watch the money. We're almost out."

"If you're watching the money, why'd you buy the razor?"
I said. "I'd rather have orange juice."

"Well, I would rather have a shave," said Jake. He
straightened up and checked his face in the mirror. "Death
Row Jethro," he said, and sank back. "She'd take one look and
run. I can't abide not shaving."

"*I* can't abide not eating fruit," I told him. "I just have
this craving; I believe I'm getting scurvy."

"Will you quit that? Will you just stop dwelling on a
thing?"

I quit. I ate some more Doritos and looked at the woods.

Once I got used to the bareness—slick brown needled floor, color washed out in the dusk—I thought it was sort of pleasant here. But Jake was so restless. He started crackling through the grocery bag. He took some Doritos after all and then brought out the Coke bottle, unscrewed the top, and sent a fine warm spray over both of us. "Oops. Sorry," he said.

"That's all right."

"Have a drink."

"No, thanks."

"If you like," he said, "you can sleep in the back tonight. I ain't sleeping anyhow. I plan to just sit here and go crazy."

"Okay."

"I don't see how you stand this," he said.

"You forget," I told him, "I've been married."

We sat there munching Doritos, watching the trees grow taller and blacker as night came on.

10

I first left my husband in 1960, after an argument over the furniture. This was Alberta's furniture that he'd stored instead of selling, for some reason, back when he sold her house. We hadn't been married a month when he hired a U-Haul and brought everything home with him: her rickety bedroom suites, linoleum-topped table and worn-out chairs, her multicolored curtains and shawls and dresses . . . add to this her father-in-law's belongings as well, all the props and costumes the old man had stashed in the dining room. Well, I thought Saul meant to hold a garage sale or something. Certainly I saw that we couldn't go on paying the storage bills. But it seemed he had no such intention. He kept it, every bit of it. The house was overstuffed as it was, so he had to double things up: an end table in front of another end table, a second sofa backed against the first. It was crazy. Every piece of furniture had its shadow, a Siamese twin. My mother didn't seem to find it odd at all (she doted on him now, she thought he could do no wrong) but I did. He wouldn't even open Alberta's letters; what did he want with her furniture?

I myself thought of Alberta daily, and had coveted all she owned for years, but these were just her cast-offs. If she had managed to fling them away, so could I. "Saul," I said, "we have to get rid of this clutter. I can't move. I can't breathe! It's got to go."

"Oh, we'll sort it out eventually," was what he said.

I believed him. I continued stumbling over crates of satin shoes and riding boots, bruising my shins in the tangle of chair legs, waiting for him to take some action. But then he started Bible College and became so preoccupied. At night he was studying, and any spare time he had was given to the radio shop. It was plain he'd forgotten that furniture utterly.

Along about October, I decided to dispose of it myself. I admit it: I went behind his back. I didn't call Goodwill in an open and aboveboard way that he would notice but snuck things out, piece by piece, and set them by the trashcan. The truck came by on Wednesdays and Saturdays. Wednesday I put out a nightstand, Saturday a bookcase. I couldn't discard more than one thing at a time because the town had a limit on bulk trash. This made me very impatient. I lay awake planning what to get rid of next; it was so hard to choose. The bureau? Or the end table? Part of me wanted to work my way through the kitchen chairs, but there were eight of them and that would be so boring, week after week. Part of me wanted to head straight for the sofa, the biggest thing in the house. But surely he would notice that. Wouldn't he?

His attitude now was fond but abstracted—not what you look for in a husband. He'd settled me so quickly into his life; he'd moved on to other projects. I felt like something dragged on a string behind a forgetful child. I couldn't understand how we'd arrived so soon at the same muddy, tangled, flawed relationship that I had with everyone else.

I began to consider all our belongings with an eye to how they would look beside the trashcan. Not just Alberta's things, but Mama's and my own as well. After all, did we really need to write at desks, walk on rugs? In the middle of dinner I would freeze, staring at the china cupboard full of compote dishes. Why, they would even fit *inside* the trashcan, not lose me a single collection day. And how about my father's Graflex that I had never used, and my baby clothes in the brassbound trunk and the files full of dead people's passport photos? What good were they to me?

Wednesday morning I made my decision: Alberta's bureau. I waited till Saul had gone to the radio shop, and then I lugged it down the stairs—first the drawers, one by one, and then the frame. The frame was hard to handle and it clumped quite a bit. My mother called from the kitchen: "Charlotte? Is that you?" I had to stop and rest the bureau on a step and steady my voice and say, "Yes, Mama."

"What's happening up there?"

"Nothing, Mama."

I took it out the front, so she wouldn't see. Dragged it around to the alley, slid all the drawers in and left it by the trashcan. Then I went to the grocery store, and on to Photo Supply for some bromide paper. So it was noon before I got home again. I stepped in the door, set down my packages, and came face to face with Alberta's bureau.

Well, it was like meeting up with a corpse that I'd already buried. I was truly startled. And it didn't help to have Saul looming behind it with his arms folded across his chest. "Why," I said. "What is *this* doing here?"

"I found it by the trashcan," he said.

"You did?"

"Luckily, it's Columbus Day and nobody picked it up."

"Oh. Columbus Day," I said.

"How many other things have you thrown away?"

"Well . . ."

"It's not yours to dispose of, Charlotte. What would make you chuck it out like that?"

"Well, I ought to have *some* say what's in this house," I told him. "And when I spoke to you about it you were too busy, oh, you couldn't be bothered with earthly things."

"I was working," said Saul. "I'm falling asleep on my books every night. I can't stop to rearrange the furniture at the drop of a hat."

"Drop of a hat! I asked you in August. But no, you had to wait for the proper moment. And then went off muttering scripture somewhere, practicing handshakes or whatever it is you do in that place, I wouldn't know."

"Naturally you wouldn't," he said, "since you didn't come to Opening Day at Hamden, where they explained it all."

"But I don't like Hamden," I told him. "I hate the whole idea, and I would try to make you quit if I were sure that I had any right to change people.'"

"Well, I don't understand you," he said.

"No, I know you don't. Preachers never ask themselves that question, that's what's wrong with them."

"What question? What are we talking about? Listen, all I want is for you to leave my things alone. Don't touch them. I'll tend to them sometime later."

"Even if they're breaking my neck?" I asked.

He brushed a hand across his forehead, like someone exhausted. "I never thought you'd turn out to be this kind of person, Charlotte," he said. "That furniture is mine, and I'll decide what to do with it. Meanwhile, I'm late for class. Goodbye."

He left, closing the door too quietly. I heard the pickup start. I gathered my packages and took them to the kitchen, where I found my mother sitting rigid in her lawn chair. These days she had packed down somewhat; she was merely a very stout, sagging woman, and could have sat anywhere she chose but returned to the lawn chair during moments of stress. She wore her old scared look and clutched the splintery arms with white-tipped fingers. I said, "Never mind, Mama. It's all right."

"You treat him so badly," she said, "and he's so fine and mannerly."

She liked Saul a lot more than she'd ever liked me.

I said, "Mama, I have to defend myself."

"But you don't want to drive him off," she said.

"Drive him off?" I said. "Ha!" It was exactly what I did want. I could see myself chasing him with a stick, like the girl on the Old Dutch Cleanser can: "Back away! Back away! Give me air!" This hopeless, powerless feeling would vanish like a fog, if I could just drive him off. I would be free then of his judging gaze that noted all my faults and sins, that widened at learning who I really was. I would be rid of his fine and mannerly presence, eternally showing me up. But I didn't say any of that to my mother. I set the packages on the counter, kissed her cheek, and left, swinging my purse. Walked across town to Libby's Grill. Ordered a bus ticket for New York City.

I believe that was the clearest, happiest moment of all my life.

But this was 1960, remember, when Clarion was still a sleepy little town and there weren't all that many buses. "What day are you leaving?" Libby asked. (In 1960, there really was a Libby still.)

I said, "Day?"

"Bus comes through Mondays and Thursdays, Charlotte. Which do you want a ticket for?"

This place just wouldn't let go of me. You'd think at least they'd get the bus schedule synchronized with the garbage schedule.

"Thursday, please," I said. "Tomorrow."

And then I had to empty out my purse. All she gave me back was eight dollars. But the ticket was worth it, I decided: long enough to tie around my waist. I folded it carefully, feeling slowed and chastened.

After that, I needed a place to stay till Thursday. It was ridiculous that Saul got to live at my mother's. And Aunt Aster would never allow her guest room to be used. In the end, I had to go on over to the Blue Moon Motel—four dollars nightly, a joke for high school boys with fast ideas. Had to spend the afternoon lying on a mangy chenille bedspread in my stocking feet, not so much as a television to watch, not even a file to do my nails with. My life grew perfectly still, but I told myself it was the stillness that animals take on just before they spring into action.

This was when they hadn't yet opened the lipstick factory, so when Saul got home from class I don't think it took him twenty minutes to track me down. Everybody knew where I'd gone; everybody'd seen me tearing off down the street on a brisk October day without a coat on. Or so they said. (Actually I'd been walking, very calmly.) Saul came to the motel and knocked on my door, two sharp knocks. "Charlotte, let me in. What's the matter with you?"

I was suddenly filled with strength. I was jubilant. I wanted to laugh.

"Charlotte!"

It was clear from the self-assured tone of his voice that he didn't know what he was up against. I refused to answer him.

After a while he went away.

Then everything buckled and crumbled. I felt so sad, I thought something inside me was breaking. I wished I could erase all I'd ever done, give up and die. So when the phone rang, I pounced on it. It was Saul. He said, "Charlotte, quit this, please."

"I'll never quit," I said.

"You want me to get a key from Mrs. Baynes and come in after you?"

"You can't, I've got the chain on the door."

"Look. I know you wouldn't leave me," he said.

"I wouldn't?"

"I know you love me."

"I don't love you at all."

"I think this must have something to do with your condition," he said.

"Condition? What condition?"

"You're pregnant. Aren't you."

"Don't be ridiculous," I told him.

"You can't fool me, I remember from when my brothers were born. *Lots* of times I . . . Charlotte?"

I was counting. I looked around for a calendar but there wasn't one. I had to count on my fingers, whispering dates to myself. Saul said, "Charlotte?"

"Oh, my God in heaven," I said.

Saul said, "Charlotte, I wish you wouldn't take the Lord's name in vain like that."

Being pregnant affected me in ways I hadn't foreseen. For one thing, I became very energetic. I would dash around the studio, shoving heavy cartons aside, wheeling that old camera on its creaky stand till the soldier or whoever rose from his chair looking anxious: "Uh, ma'am, do you think this is wise?" I was stronger and needed less sleep. Long into the night sometimes I'd be pacing the floor. But I was also easily hurt, and things could make me cry for no reason. Julian, for instance.

Julian was Saul's youngest brother, the handsomest and most shiftless of all. He had a sulky, rumpled, Italian look that used to charm all the girls in school, and his weakness was gambling. But gambling men are not as dashing as the folk songs make them out to be; they tend to break down when they're on a losing streak. Julian showed up at our door one morning unwashed, ragged, with a string of bad checks trailing clear back to Texas. He fell into one of Alberta's old beds and slept a week, waking only for meals. When finally he got up he seemed purified, like somebody recovering from a fever. He said he would do anything—change his ways completely, make up every cent he owed. He started work at the radio shop, and Saul wrote on Bible School stationery to everybody holding one of Julian's bad checks, promising to send the money as soon as we had it.

On my daily walk that the doctor had ordered, I would pass the radio shop and see Julian bent low over tubes and wires, dimmed by a picture window as grainy as an old photograph. In the well of this window was the same display they'd had when I was a child: a plastic knob, a twist of wastepaper, and the dusty innards of an RCA Victor phonograph. I wanted to go in and pull Julian out of there. I almost did, sometimes.

But Julian said he had settled down, was here forever, planned to join the church, even. "In Texas," he said one night, "I thought about church a lot. I thought about those songs they sing, all those hymns I never used to care for. One morning I woke up in jail, not even knowing how I'd landed there, and I said to myself, 'If I get out of this I'm going back where I came from, join the church and straighten out my life. Going to stay with my brother till I die of old age,' I said to myself."

I looked at Saul.

"You tell them that on Sunday," Saul said.

"I got to know a few of the prisoners. Why, they'd been in and out of jail all their lives, had no hope any more. Know how they passed the time? They'd chew up their bread and make it into statues, get the guards to sell it outside."

"Stop," I said.

"Little statues of Donald Duck, Minnie Mouse, people like that. Little chewed-up statues."

"I don't want to hear about this," I said, and started crying. Everybody stared at me. "Why, Charlotte," said Saul, and my mother fumbled at her bosom for a Kleenex.

I really was very peculiar during those months.

Our daughter was born June 2, 1961, at the Clarion County Hospital, where I refused all anesthesia including aspirin so I could be absolutely sure nobody mixed her up with any other baby. We named her Catherine. She had fair skin and light brown hair, but her face was Saul's.

From the first, it was clear she was bright. She did everything early: sitting, crawling, walking. She put short words together before she was one, and not much later began to tell herself long secret stories at bedtime. When she was two, she invented a playmate named Selinda. I knew that was normal, and didn't worry about it. I apologized when I stepped on Selinda's toes, and set a place for her at every meal. But after a while, Catherine moved to Selinda's place and left her own place empty. She said she had a friend named Catherine that none of us could see. Eventually she stopped talking about Catherine. We seemed to be left with Selinda. We have had Selinda with us ever since. Now that I think of it, I might as well have taken that anesthesia after all.

They have this free offer on the radio sometimes: you send them a self-addressed envelope and they'll send you a pamphlet called "What If Christ Had Never Come?" That always makes me laugh. I can think of a lot we'd have missed if Christ had never come. The Spanish Inquisition, for one thing. For another, losing my husband to the Hamden Bible College.

Oh, I did lose him. He wasn't the old Saul Emory. He'd adopted a whole new set of rules, attitudes, platitudes, judgments; he didn't even need to think. In any situation, all he had to do was rest back on his easy answers. He could reach for his religion and pull it around him like his preacher's robe.

When I was in the hospital having Selinda, Reverend Davitt lay dying one floor above me. (Lung cancer: one of God's little jokes. Reverend Davitt didn't hold with tobacco.) By the fall of '61, Saul was pastor of Holy Basis. He wouldn't be ordained till June but already had his own little flock, his tarpaper church and cubby-sized office where people could discuss with him their various forms of unhappiness. What's more, he said he would like me to start attending the services now. I refused. I told him I had my rights; and he said, yes, I did, but he hoped I would come anyway because it was very important to him.

Well, I went. That first Sunday I left Selinda in the preschool room downstairs and sat in a pew between Julian and my mother. I wore a powder-blue suit, a pillbox hat, little white gloves. For the sake of the congregation, I tried to look as rapt as I was expected to. I tried not to show my shock when Saul came out in his robes like a stranger and read the morning's scripture in a firm, authoritative voice. Older members of the congregation said, "Amen"; the others merely kept a hushed silence. Then we all stood up and sang a hymn. We resettled ourselves and Saul arranged various papers on his pulpit. "I have here," he said finally, "a clipping from last Wednesday's newspaper: 'Dr. Tate's Answer Column.'"

His words echoed slightly, as if spoken in a train station.

"'Dear Dr. Tate: I am writing about this problem I have in talking with my physician. I mention this to show what I think of physicians and how much they expect of a person. Every Thursday my doctor has me come in to see him and he wonders why my diabetes is always getting worse. I tell him I just don't know. Well, Dr. Tate, the fact is that I do eat quite a bit of pastry that I don't admit to. I just get this urge to stuff sometimes. Also I overdo on the wine. I know that wine isn't really liquor but I feel bad anyway drinking in the daytime and so I don't tell him. Dr. Tate, my husband doesn't love me any more and goes with someone else and my only son died of a bone disease when he was barely three years old. I weigh two hundred and thirty-one pounds and my skin's all broken out though they say that stops at twenty and I am forty-four. Yet somehow I can't tell any of this to my doctor and do you know why? Because a doctor sets himself up so and acts like he won't even like you if you eat the wrong kind of nutrition. So how does he think I could admit all this to him? And what I want to ask anyway is, Where's the *fairness* to this, Dr. Tate?' "

I was interested. I folded my gloves and looked up at Saul, waiting for Dr. Tate's answer. But instead of reading it, Saul laid the clipping aside and gazed out over his congregation. "The woman who wrote that letter," he told them, "is not alone. She could be you or me. She lives in fear of disapproval, in a world where love is conditional. She wonders what the point is. The only one she can think of to ask is a licensed physician.

"Is this what we've come to, finally? Are we so far removed from God?"

I yawned, and wove the fingers of my gloves together.

That was the last sermon of Saul's I ever listened to.

Which is not to say I didn't go to church. Oh, no, I showed up every Sunday morning, sitting between my mother and Julian, smiling my glazed wifely smile. I believe I almost enjoyed it; I took some pleasure in his distance, in my own dreamy docility and my private, untouchable deafness. His words slipped past me like the sound of a clock or an ocean. Meanwhile I watched his hands gripping the pulpit, I admired his chiseled lips. Plotted how to get him into bed with me. There was something magical about that pew that sent all my thoughts swooning toward bed. Contrariness, I suppose. He was against making love on a Sunday. I was in favor of it. Sometimes I won, sometimes he won. I wouldn't have missed Sunday for the world.

I had a lot of foolish hopes, those first few years. I imagined that one day he might lose his faith, just like that, and go on to something new. Join a motorcycle gang. Why not? We'd travel everywhere, Selinda and I perched behind him. I would be hugging his waist, laying my cheek against his black cloth back.

Black cloth?

Oh, it was ingrained, by now: even on a motorcycle, he'd be wearing his seedy suit and carrying his Bible. He would never stop being a preacher. And even if he did, I wasn't so sure any more that it would make a difference.

Often Saul invited people for Sunday dinner—homeless visitors, sinners from the mourners' bench. Sometimes they stayed. We had an old lady named Miss Feather, for instance, up on our third floor—evicted from her apartment the spring of '63, just borrowing a room until she found another. Which she never did. Never will, I suppose. We had soldiers, hitchhikers, traveling salesmen—country people lonesome for their family churches, passing through, glad for a taste of my buckwheat pancakes. And one Sunday, a bearded man in work clothes came to the mourners' bench while the congregation was singing "Just As I Am." Saul stopped his singing and descended from the pulpit. He set his hands on the man's shoulders. Then he hugged him, gripping the dark, shiny head which was—why, of course! An Emory head. Linus Emory, the one who'd had the nervous breakdown, freed by his aunt's death to wander back. Depressed as ever, but lit by this reunion like a bone china cup held up to a candle. We took him home for dinner. He spent all the mealtime looking around the table at us, staring into Selinda's face, hanging on our words so closely

that he almost seemed to be speaking them with us. Even Mama
—even old Miss Feather, passing him the beaten biscuits—
could make his eyes too shiny. It was so good to be home, he
told us. Then he went upstairs and claimed another of Alberta's
old beds, and unpacked his cardboard suitcase into a bureau.

Are you keeping track? There were seven of us now, not
counting those just passing through. Amos was still in Iowa,
teaching music, I believe. And Alberta was someplace in California. But otherwise we'd transplanted that house of theirs
lock, stock, and barrel. We had their beds, their hats, their
sons, their one-way window eyes. Even my mother appeared to
have solidified into someone darker, and Miss Feather had
taken on their proud way of standing, and Selinda's face was as
seraphic as something in a locket. "Have you noticed?" I asked
Saul. "There seem to be so many Emorys here."

But Saul only nodded, thumbing through his datebook, no
doubt hunting another funeral or Youth Group meeting. "I
always did want a place for my brothers to come home to," he
said.

That was what he'd always wanted?

Oh, I saw it now. Finally I could sum him up: he'd only
been a poor, homesick G.I., longing for house, wife, family,
church. A common type. Every mourners' bench has one.
"You're just looking for a way not to be alone," I told him.

But Saul said, "There *is* no way not to be alone," and shut
his datebook and looked out across the dark hallway. Then I
was unsure again, and saw that I couldn't sum him up after all.
Whatever he was once, it had taken me all these years to find it
out and now I couldn't say what he was today. I would be
several steps behind forever.

"And the—and the money!" I cried, to keep from being
drawn to him. "How can we feed them?" (Thinking meanwhile
of the shallow brass collection plates, his only income; of the
nickel-and-dime studio; and the radio shop that barely paid

Julian's gambling debts, which shrank and swelled like something alive according to his lapses.)

"The Lord will provide," said Saul. He left for his meeting.

I gave up hope. Then in order not to mind too much I loosened my roots, floated a few feet off, and grew to look at things with a faint, pleasant humorousness that spiced my nose like the beginnings of a sneeze. After a while the humor became a habit; I couldn't have lost it even if I'd tried. My world began to seem . . . temporary. I saw that I must be planning to leave, eventually. Surely I wouldn't be with him very much longer. At all times now I carried a hundred-dollar traveler's check in the secret compartment of my billfold. I had bought my walking shoes. I planned to take nothing else but Selinda—my excess baggage, loved and burdensome. When would the proper current come to bear us away?

In the studio, sometimes, I found myself stopping work as if to listen for its arrival, raising my head and growing dazed and still. Then the customer would clear his throat or shuffle his feet, and I would say, "Hmm?" and quickly wheel closer the camera that I still didn't think of as my own. It was my father's. This was his room. Those were his yellowed, brittle prints curling off the walls. I was only a transient. My photos were limpid and relaxed, touched with that grace things have when you know they're of no permanent importance.

11

The Dorothea Whitman Home was a mansion on a hill, landscaped, framed by trees. "Sheesh!" Jake said, peering at it through the windshield. We had parked at the gateposts, which were topped with spongy stone balls. It was six o'clock in the morning, and both of us were half asleep and chilled through. Also, we hadn't had breakfast yet. We *could* have, but Jake had spent the time shaving instead. He had shaved without water and his face had a new, raw, inadequate look. I thought we'd have done much better going to a Toddle House. And there wasn't a sign of Mindy Callender.

"Now, here is what she told me," said Jake. "Said, 'Park at the gatepost and I'll come on down.' Well, ain't this a gatepost? Ain't it?"

"Looks like one to *me*," I said.

"Maybe she meant the front door."

"Why would she call the front door a gatepost?"

"But if she has to make a fast getaway, see. Then we ought to be parked a mite nearer."

"I would stay by the gatepost," I said.

"Well, I tell you this much," said Jake. "Five minutes more and I'm going. I can think of lots of places I'd rather be than here."

High on the hill, the great scrolled door of the mansion opened and someone stepped out. From this far away she looked like one of those little figures in a weather house. Her stomach was circular, flower-shaped, preceding the rest of her by a good two feet. She wore a straw hat and a pink dress, and carried a suitcase and a bundle of something dark. While she was walking toward us she never once looked in our direction, but picked her way carefully with her head lowered so that all we saw was the crown of her hat. "Is that Mindy?" I asked Jake.

"Naw, it's the warden."

"Well, *I* don't know what Mindy looks like."

"It's Mindy, all right," he said. "She never did dress like she had any common sense."

For she was close enough now so that we could see what she was wearing: a print sundress not meant for anyone so pregnant, with straps as thin as the joint lines on a Barbie Doll's shoulders. Her hat was ringed with little embroidered hearts. The bundle in her arms turned out to be a cat. "Cripes, a cat!" Jake said.

Mindy raised her head then and looked at us. She had a childish round face with a pointed chin, and white-blond hair that streamed to her waist. Some ten feet from the car she stopped and set her suitcase down, not smiling. "Well," Jake sighed, and he opened the door and got out. "Hey there, Mindy," he called.

"Who's that you got with you."

"Hmm?"

"Who's that *lady,* Jake?"

"Oh, why, she's just going to ride with us a spell," Jake said. "Get on in, now."

"How'm I going to get in with the doors chained shut?"

"Use my side. Move it, Mindy, they'll be after you."

"Oh, everybody's still sleeping," Mindy said. She came around the car, lugging the suitcase stiff-armed and just barely hanging on to her cat. Jake drew away from her, but without actually stepping back.

"Now I am not going to drive no *cat* about," he told her.

"But he's mine."

"Look here, Mindy."

"He *belongs* to me."

Jake rubbed his nose. "Okay, okay," he said. "Make sure he stays in your lap, though." He opened the back door, shoved her suitcase in, and stood aside to let her follow it. Mindy stayed where she was. "Aren't I going to sit in the front?" she asked him.

"How come?"

"We been separated all these months and now you want to ask how *come?*"

She stood on tiptoe suddenly and twined her free arm around his neck. She really was a tiny girl. The biggest thing about her was that stomach, which Jake carefully wasn't looking at. "We got a lot of plans to make," she said, and kissed the corner of his mouth. Then she slid into the car, bounced a little, and turned to me. "I'm Mindy Callender," she told me.

"I'm Charlotte Emory."

"Pee-ew! Where'd this old car come from? Smells like a dustbin."

Maybe it did, but all I could smell was her perfume: sugared strawberries. As soon as Jake had settled in the driver's seat, he rolled down the window a crack. "Won't you be cold?" I asked Mindy.

"Oh no, I've got the hot flashes."

"The what?"

"Been hot as Hades the whole seven months. Can't stand a blanket, won't wear sweaters. It only happens with some rare few women." She cast a sudden look at Jake, who didn't say anything. He started the car and set off down the road. "What's that funny noise?" Mindy asked him.

"What noise?"

"Jake, I just don't know about this car. Where'd you say you got it?"

"Off a friend," Jake said.

"Some friend."

She settled back, hugging the cat. This cat was a marbled brown color, with glaring yellow eyes and chipped ears. It was plain he didn't like to be held. First he tried to struggle free and then he gave up, but not really: his eyes were squared, the tip of his tail twitched, and every time Mindy patted him he would shrug her off. "I believe that Plymouth would rather he hadn't come," said Mindy.

Jake said, "Who?"

"Plymouth. My cat."

"Well, I go along with Plymouth," said Jake. "What you want a cat for? You never used to like them."

"At the Home there's a pet for everyone," Mindy told him. "They say it's therapeutic."

"Therapeutic."

"Some of the girls have dogs. Some have birds."

"Well, I don't hold with having birds," said Jake.

"We make things, too; that's therapeutic. And we have a lot of activities, speeches and lessons and things. Last night we had Child Care; that's why I couldn't meet you. We were going to give a bath to a rubber doll and I didn't want to miss it."

Jake slammed on the brakes, though the highway was deserted. He turned and stared at Mindy. "Watch the *road*, Jake," Mindy said.

"Now, let me get this straight," said Jake. "You couldn't meet us last evening because you had to give a doll a bath."

"Well, there was a lot of other stuff too," Mindy said.

"Mindy Callender, do you know where we spent last night? Sleeping out. Shut in a car in the middle of the woods, and with no hot flashes to warm us, neither."

"Well, who is 'us'?" Mindy asked.

"Me and Charlotte, who'd you think?"

She gave me a closer look. Deep down, her eyes were speckled. "I didn't quite catch it," she said. "*Where* is it you come from?"

"Clarion," said Jake.

"She been riding all this way with you?"

"She's, ah, going as far as Florida," Jake told her. "Then she'll be saying goodbye."

"Florida! Oh, Jake, is that where we're headed?" And she rose up to hug him, covering my lap with a billow of skirts, pulling Jake sideways. The car swerved. The cat made a leap and landed in the back seat, shaking various parts of himself and looking insulted.

"Watch it, will you," Jake said. "Well, I figure we might as well be *warm* the next two months, no harm in that. Besides, Oliver's in Florida."

"Oh, Oliver, Oliver, always Oliver," said Mindy, picking brown hairs off her dress. Now that the cat was gone I could see that she also had a purse: shiny white vinyl, heart-shaped, like something a child would carry to Sunday School. She caught me looking at it and spun it by its strap. "Like it?" she asked me. "It's new."

"It's very nice," I said.

"I thought it would match my other stuff."

She raised a thin, knobby wrist, with a bracelet dangling heart-shaped charms in all different colors and sizes. The pink stone in her ring was heart-shaped too, and so was the print of her dress. "Hearts are my *sign,*" Mindy said. "What's yours?"

"Well, I don't really have a sign," I told her.

"You married, Charlotte?"

"Of course she's married, leave off of her," Jake said.

"I was just asking."

"She don't want all your busybody questions."

"Look here, Jake, we were just having this ordinary conversation about my purse and all, and the only thing I asked her was—"

"You got any money in that purse?" Jake said.

"Huh? I don't know. A little, I guess."

"How much?"

"Well, talk about busybody!"

"See, I left home without my wallet," Jake said.

"How could you do a thing like that?"

"Never mind how, it just happened that way. How much you got?"

Mindy opened her purse and riffled through it. "Ten, fifteen . . . sixteen dollars and some cents, it looks like."

"That ain't very much," said Jake.

"Well, la-de-da to *you,* mister."

We passed a truckful of crated chickens. There was a silence. Then Jake said, "They let you carry money around that place?"

"Sure."

"But what would you use it for?"

"Oh, like if we want to walk into town or something. Buy us a soda or shampoo or movie magazine."

"You just walk on into town," said Jake. "Any old time you want."

"What's wrong with that?"

I took tight hold of the door handle and waited. But Jake didn't say a thing, not a word. He merely drove on, with his face as still as a stone.

In the restroom of the diner where we stopped for breakfast, Mindy had me put her hair into ponytails. "I was scared to do it myself," she said, "and my roommate was asleep."

"What were you scared of?" I asked.

"Why, you know I shouldn't raise my arms that high. I might strangle the baby on its cord."

"But—"

"How do I look?" she asked me.

She looked about twelve years old, younger than my daughter even, with her two perky ponytails and her blue, trusting gaze. In the mirror beside her I was suddenly dimmed: an older woman, flat-haired, wearing a raincoat that had clearly been slept in. "Don't you have no lipstick?" Mindy said.

"Lipstick? No."

"Well, maybe you'd like to borrow mine."

She handed it to me, already unrolled—something pink and fruity-smelling. I handed it back. "Thanks anyway," I told her.

"Come on, you could use a little color."

"No, really, I—"

"You want me to do it?"

"No. Please."

"But listen, at the Home I made up everybody. I mean a lot of those girls just never had learned what to do with theirselves, you know? Keep still a minute."

"*Stop!*" I said.

She looked startled. She took a step backward, still holding the lipstick.

"Oh, I'm sorry," I told her.

"That's all right," she said. She rolled and capped the lipstick in silence, and dropped it into her purse. "Well!" she said. But when she looked up again I saw that her face was white and stricken, smaller somehow than before.

"Please don't feel bad," I told her. "It's just that I didn't want to be put in someone else's looks. I mean," I said, trying to make a joke of it, "what if I got *stuck* that way? Like crossing your eyes; didn't your mother ever warn you about that?"

Mindy said, "Oh, Charlotte, do you think he's at all glad to see me?"

"Of course he is," I said.

Driving was slower now because we had to stop so often. First of all, the cat kept getting carsick. From time to time he would give this low moan, and then Jake would curse and brake and swerve to the side of the road. The trouble was, the cat wouldn't come out of the car then. We'd all be calling, "Plymouth? Here, Plymouth," but he only crouched down beneath the seat, and we'd have to sit helpless and listen to his little choking sounds. "This is *therapeutic?*" Jake asked.

Then Mindy had so many foot cramps. Every time one hit her, we'd have to stop and let her walk it off. We stood leaning against the car, watching her hobble through some field littered with flowers and beer bottles. It was truly warm now, and so bright I had to squint. Mindy looked like a little sunlit robot.

"It's easing!" she would call back. "I feel it starting to ease up some!"

"Now's the kind of time I wish I smoked," Jake said.

"I can feel those muscles slacking!"

Jake's jacket ballooned in the wind. He slouched beside me. Our elbows touched. We were like two parents exercising a child in the park. "*You* had children," he said suddenly, as if reading my mind.

I nodded.

"Ever get foot cramps?"

"Well, no."

"It's all in her head," he told me.

"Oh, I doubt that."

I could feel him watching me. I looked away. Then he asked, "How many?"

"What?"

"How many children."

"Two," I said.

"Your husband like kids?"

"Well, of course."

"What's he do?"

"Do?"

"Do for a *living,* Charlotte. Where's your mind at?"

"Oh. He's a . . . well, he's a preacher," I said.

Jake whistled.

"You're putting me on," he told me.

"No."

Mindy wandered back to us, trailing strands of flowers. "They're gone now," she said. But Jake only looked at her blankly, as if wondering what it was that was supposed to have gone.

Along about noontime, we passed a billboard showing a clump of plastic oranges, welcoming us to Florida. "Whoopee!" Mindy said. "Now, how much further?"

"Forever," Jake told her. "Ain't you ever seen a U.S. map? We are driving down its great old long big toe."

"But I'm tired of riding. Can't we stop at a motel or something? Miss Bohannon says long drives aren't good for us."

"Who's Miss Bohannon?"

"She's a nurse, she teaches Child Care."

Jake frowned and speeded up. "Well, another thing," he said. "I don't *understand* why they have this Child Care business."

"To tell how to care for a child, silly."

"Seems kind of pointless, if you ask me," Jake said. "You know most of them girls will just put their kids out for adoption."

"Sure, but they're not the ones that take the course," said Mindy. "They take Good Grooming."

"Ah," Jake said. He drove along a while. Some thought worked through his forehead. He took his foot off the gas pedal. "Wait," he said.

"Hmm?"

"Are you telling me you're going to keep this kid?"

"Well, naturally."

"Now, listen. I don't think that's such a very good idea."

"Why . . . Jake? You're not saying we should just . . ."

"*We?*"

Mindy turned and looked at me. I stared hard at a passing Shell station.

"What you getting at, Mindy?" Jake asked. "Are you trying to plan on us marrying, or something?"

"Of course I plan on it," Mindy said. "Otherwise what did you drive all this way for? You must have cared a *little* bit, to come so far."

"Well, I'm only human," said Jake. "I mean, even when they hijack a plane, they let the kids go free. Even when they're fighting for lifeboats, they put the kids in first."

"Lifeboats? What? What're you talking about?"

"I come to get a baby out of prison," Jake said. "Ha! Some prison. Seems you told me a bald-faced lie."

"It wasn't a lie! How can you say that? Now listen here, Jake Simms," Mindy said. "You're not backing out of this. You come all this way, take me out of the Home, transport me to another state—and now you're going to change your mind? No sir. We're going to get married and have a little baby, and the prettiest home you ever heard of."

"Not ever in a million, billion years," said Jake.

"Why, we could stay right here in Florida, if you like. Get a little place near Oliver, wouldn't that be nice? Really the climate would be better for the children," she said, turning to me. "I mean, they won't get so many colds and all, we won't have to buy all those snowsuits. It's cheaper. And I've always been a warm-weather person. I'll make the house real summery, lots of bright colors, straw chairs, those ruffly white curtains with the tie-backs, you know the kind, what do you call them?"

"Priscillas," I said.

"Priscillas. That's what we'll have. Priscillas. Everywhere but the living room; I think there we'll have fiberglass drapes of some type. Gold, you know, or maybe avocado. Which would you rather, Jake. Gold?"

Jake stared straight ahead of him.

"Avocado?"

The scenery slid past us: used boat lots, real estate offices, praline shops. Everything looked untidy. If this was Florida I didn't like it at all. I didn't even like the way the sun shone here, so flat and white, burdening the tinny roofs of the roadside stands.

"Jake, I got this cramp again," Mindy said in a small voice.

Jake didn't so much as change expression. He just pulled over and stopped the car. From beneath the back seat, the cat gave a yowl. Jake got out and the two of us slid after him. We were on the edge of a shambling little town called Pariesto, according to the signs. Mindy had nowhere to walk but the littered gravel at the side of the road—white-hot, mica-laden, dazzling to the eyes. She stalked off anyway, very fast, with her hands joined under her stomach.

"Now, don't you dare say I should go after her," Jake told me.

I was surprised. "Me?" I said.

"Isn't that what women do? 'Oh, go after her, Jake. Go see if you can help.' "

"But—I haven't opened my mouth," I said.

"You were about to."

"I was not!"

Mindy stumbled in her little sandals. She went down on one knee.

"Go after her," Jake told me.

I ran and caught up with her. By the time I arrived she was on her feet again. "Mindy?" I said. "Are you all right?"

"Oh, yes," she said, brushing at her skirt. She kept her eyes lowered; her lashes were long and white, clumsily tipped with little blotches of mascara. "I'm supposed to just point my heels," she said. "That's what helps the cramps. If I just, like, jab my heels in the gravel, here . . ."

She stopped and looked up at me. "Charlotte," she said, "it wasn't a lie. Can't you explain to him? He doesn't understand. I mean, it really is a prison if you got no place else to go to. Isn't it?"

"Well, naturally," I said. "You want to turn around now?"

"I just don't have any choice; he'll have to go through with this," she said, letting me lead her back. "It's not any picnic for *me*, you know. Long about the fifth or sixth month, why, I got so mad and so tired of waiting for him I believe I just stopped loving him. I really believe I might not love him any more. But what else is there for me to do?"

We walked along the strip of gravel, wading through cellophane bags and candy wrappers. Jake had got back in the car to wait for us, I saw. He was sitting in the passenger seat, with his head bowed low and buried in his hands.

From Pariesto on, Mindy did the driving. She said it helped her foot cramps. I sat in my usual place, and Jake moved to the middle. Although it was hot now, he kept his jacket on and his collar up, as if for protection. The wind ruffled his hair into loose damp curls and turned my face stiff and salty. Only Mindy, working on her own peculiar little thermostat, seemed comfortable. She kept her elbows out and her chin up, and drove at a fast, smooth pace that gradually raised her spirits. Before long, she was humming. Then she started singing. She sang "Love Will Keep Us Together." When her accelerator foot began beating in rhythm, Jake said, "You want to cool it a little?" But the rest of the time he let her do as she pleased. He slid down in his seat, with his arms folded across his chest and his head tilted back. I would have said he was asleep, if I hadn't looked closely and seen the gray slits of his eyes.

Late in the afternoon, in a town I didn't catch the name of, we stopped at a Woolworth's. Mindy wanted to get a glass of milk at the soda fountain. She said she had to have at least a quart a day. "Yeah, well," Jake said, "but the way I figure it, we're not but a couple of hours from Perth. Can't you hold out till then?"

"It's not for me, it's for the baby," Mindy told him. "If it was for me I could hold out forever. I hate milk. You coming?"

She stepped from the car in a swirl of pink, and we followed her into Woolworth's. This was an *old* Woolworth's, with creaky dark floors and a smell of popcorn. There were counters full of Spray-Net, eyelash curlers, harlequin reading glasses, and mustard-seed pendants—objects I thought had vanished long ago. Mindy got waylaid by a salt-and-pepper set shaped like kerosene lanterns, and stopped to buy it. I expected Jake to hurry her but he didn't. He just stood there with his hands in his pockets, his face slack and lifeless, gazing at a Batman comic on the floor. Then we went on to the soda fountain where Mindy ordered her milk. "Ugh," she said when it came. "It's so white. It's so thick." The waitress took offense and flounced off, slapping things with a dishrag as she went. "Well, this is for *your* sake, Elton," Mindy said, and she patted her stomach and started drinking, one sip at a time. "We're naming him for Elton John," she told me. Jake studied a picture of a gray milkshake and a pink plastic hot dog from the forties. I flipped through someone's cast-off newspaper hunting "Peanuts," but even after I found it it didn't make me laugh.

When we got back to the street, we were blinded for a moment. Everything was so hot and bright, and a herd of strange, long-legged motorcycles built like praying mantises was glittering past. Jake wiped his face on his sleeve. "Next time, remind me to get a *air*-conditioned car," he told me. "This one here will be a hundred and fifty degrees inside."

As if he had sounded some alarm, Mindy cried, "Oh, no!" and started running.

"What'd I say?" Jake asked me.

I shrugged.

Mindy was tugging at the car doors—first the chained ones, then the others. She fell down out of sight. When we came around to the driver's side she was on the floor in back, reaching under both seats, patting the dusty carpeting. "Plymouth? Plymouth?"

"We left the windows open," I told Jake.

"You left *yours* open," she said, straightening up. A smudge of dirt crossed the bridge of her nose, and her hair was fraying out of its ponytails. "I closed mine up tight as a bubble, do you think I'd forget a thing like that?"

"Oh, Mindy, I'm sorry," I said, "but I'm certain we can—"

"Shoot, he'd have died of heat anyway if we'd have shut all the windows," Jake said. "You can't blame Charlotte here."

"I blame you both. I blame the two of you. You didn't neither one of you want him along anyhow. Plymouth? Oh, what'll he do now? In this town he's never laid eyes on before? Why, he might not even have caught on he was going anyplace, buried beneath the seat like he was. What must he be thinking now, coming out the window to find everything's different?"

"Why, Mindy," Jake said, "I just know he'll be all—"

"You don't know a blasted thing," she told him. "Now I want you and her to go hunt that cat and be quick about it, you hear?"

She slapped the pavement with her sandal. A pale blue vein stood out along her neck. Jake's mouth dropped. "Mindy?" he said. "What's got into you?"

But she wouldn't answer.

"You've changed, Mindy. You've turned real mean and hard, seems like."

"Yes, maybe I have," she said, "But it's you that helped cause it, Jake Simms. I didn't go and do it all alone."

They looked at each other. They were so still I could hear them breathing.

Then Jake said, "Well, the . . . cat, I guess I better hunt the cat. You coming, Charlotte?"

"All right," I said.

We started up the sidewalk, leaving Mindy behind in case the cat returned on his own. We stooped to peer under each parked car for Plymouth's lantern eyes. "Does he know his name, do you think?" I asked Jake.

"Everything's gathering in on me," he said.

I took his arm. We passed a few more cars, but didn't glance under them. We came to the end of the block and stood still, gazing into a travel agent's window to our left. "Now there is a sport I just never have tried," he said finally. He was looking at a skiing poster. "You ever skied?"

"Not even once," I said. "I always wanted to, though."

"You reckon it's dangerous?"

"Well, a little, maybe."

"I got a feeling I'd be good at it," he told me. "I know that sounds conceited."

"Maybe we should have gone north instead of south," I said.

"Someplace cold."

"Someplace with clear, cold air."

"Well," Jake said, sighing.

"Well."

Then I had a thought. "Listen," I said. "What if someone's picked Plymouth up?"

"Picked him up?"

"I mean, he could be miles away from here by now. He
could be half a county over."

"That's so," Jake said. "Why, sure. He could be anywhere! And glad to get there, too. It's no use hunting further."

We separated and walked back to the car. Mindy was
leaning against the door. At this distance she seemed older, less
hopeful. She was staring at her feet, and from the way she
slumped I guessed she had one of those late-pregnancy back-
aches. I don't think she had really expected that we would find
her cat. She barely raised her eyes when we came up. "Now,
Mindy—" Jake began, but she shooed his words away wearily
and straightened, hoisting her belly with both hands. "We might
as well get going," she said.

We settled in our familiar places. Mine seemed worn to
the shape of my body by now. I knew exactly where to put my
feet so as not to tip over the cup of melted ice on the floor. Jake
laid his arm across the back of Mindy's seat. "That cat wasn't
happy with us anyhow," he told her. "This way is better. Don't
you think?"

Mindy didn't answer. She set her jaw, frowned straight
ahead, and went into reverse. We hit a car parked a full space
behind us. Jake removed his arm. "All right, you're doing just
fine there," he said. "Now you want to go forward, I believe.
Give this guy here a signal to let him know you're coming."

Mindy unrolled her window and trailed one hand out like
a limp, used ribbon. The car drifted into the street, went
through a yellow light, proceeded several blocks in an aimless,
haphazard manner. Jake shifted his weight. "Uh, Mindy—" he
said.

We arrived at a striped sawhorse, set square across the street. Two policemen guarded it with their arms folded, their backs to us. They had a beefy, stubborn way of standing. Holsters and radios and official-looking cases dangled from their belts, all the same grainy black leather. "Lord God," said Jake. At the last minute, Mindy stopped the car. "Go around," Jake told her. "Back up. Run them down. Make a U-turn."

"Huh?" said Mindy.

"You can't do that," I said to Jake, "it's a one-way street. Sit still and enjoy the parade."

"Parade?"

A white-and-gold drum major pranced across our windshield, pronging the air with his silver baton. Brassy music bleated behind him. "Oh, *parade,*" said Jake.

Mindy started crying. The two of us looked over at her. "Mindy?" Jake said.

"It's all arranged against me!" she wailed. "Nothing will ever come out like I have dreamed! We'll *never* get to Florida!"

She bent her head to the steering wheel, both arms circling it. She cried out loud, like a child. But we could only hear her during pauses in "King of the Road," which was bearing down on us from someplace to the west. "Mindy, what *is* it?" Jake asked her. "You feel all right?"

She shook her head.

"You don't have pains or nothing."

"I have pains all over," she said. Her voice was muffled, hollow as a bell. "I'm only young! I can't do this all by myself!"

Jake reached over and cut off the ignition. The car shuddered and died. "King of the Road" had won, it seemed. It sailed above everything. The band strutted by us, high school kids, skinny little Adam's-appled boys and sweaty girls. But Mindy's head was still on the steering wheel, and Jake was turned in my direction as if he expected something from me. He said, "Charlotte, can't you help me here?"

I never know what's needed. I gave him a Kleenex from my purse.

"Well, thanks a lot," he said.

I said, "Or maybe a . . . do you want me to go get some water?"

He looked at Mindy, who only went on crying. I don't know how I could have brought water anyway; the street was packed by now. Cars had drawn up all around us and behind us. People were getting out and sitting on their fenders in their shirtsleeves. A man came by with a whole fat tree of balloons. "Would you like a balloon?" I asked Mindy.

"Charlotte, for mercy's sake," Jake said. "Can't you do no better than that?"

"Well, I was only . . . *Selinda* would have," I said. But that wasn't the truth. Selinda wouldn't have liked a balloon either. The truth was that I was grieving for Jake and Mindy both, and I didn't know who I felt sadder for. I hate a situation where you can't say clearly that one person's right and one is wrong. I was cowardly; I chose to watch the parade. A team of Clydesdales clopped past with a beer wagon, and my eyes followed their billowing feet in a long restful journey of their own. The Clydesdales left great beehives of manure. I enjoyed noticing that. There are times when these little details can draw you on like spirals up a mountain, leading you miles.

Next came a flank of majorettes, and a flowered lady who tripped alongside them with a vanity case. "Watch those feet, girls!" she kept calling. "Turd ahead!" The majorettes might have been eyeless under their visored hats, but they sidestepped neatly when necessary. The soldiers were braver and slogged straight through. A little black boy marched beside them, carrying a grownup's crutch like a rifle and swinging one rubbery arm, laughing and rolling his eyes at his friends. I had never in all my life seen anybody more delighted with himself.

"Now, where'd that Kleenex walk off to?" Jake asked me.

"Here's another," I said.

"Mindy? You ought to sit up and take notice, Mindy; they got a big float with a beauty queen on it. Top Touch sausage meat. *I've* eaten Top Touch before."

Mindy hiccuped but didn't raise her head. Jake looked over at me. "Well, what have I got to do?" he asked.

"Um . . ."

"*You're* supposed to know all this junk, what have I got to do?"

"Oh, it's *Founder's* Day," I said.

"Huh?"

I pointed to a tiny old lady with long blond hair, wearing a miniskirt, carrying a poster. FOUNDER'S DAY 1876–1976, it said, above four men's pencil-drawn faces with much-erased mouths. ONE HUNDRED YEARS OF PROGRESS.

"Well, I knew it wasn't no standard holiday," said Jake. "Lord, look at her hairdo. Reckon it's real?"

"It couldn't be. It's a wig. Saran or something," I said.

"Dynel, maybe. That's what my sister's got, Dynel."

Mindy sat up, wiping her face with the backs of her hands. Muddy gray tear tracks ran down her cheeks and her mascara had turned her raccoon-eyed. "Mindy!" Jake said. "Want a Lifesaver? Want some chewing gum?"

She shook her head.

"I believe we got some Fritos left."

"I don't want your old Fritos, Jake Simms. I want to lie down and die."

"Oh, now, don't say that. Look, I'm trying my best here. Want me to do a magic trick? I do magic tricks," he told me. "I bet you didn't know that."

"I believe you mentioned it," I said, watching a float of chubby men in fezzes.

"I'm right good, aren't I, Mindy? Tell her."

Mindy mumbled something to the steering wheel.

"What's that, Mindy? Speak up, I can't hear you."

Mindy tilted her chin. "He makes things disappear," she told the windshield.

"Right," said Jake.

"He makes things vanish into nowhere. He undoes things. Houdini is his biggest hero."

"Now at the moment I don't have no equipment," said Jake. "But bearing that in mind, Mindy, you just name any trick your heart desires and I will see what I can do. I mean that. Remember how you like magic?"

She didn't answer. He looked over at me. His face was damp from the heat of the car, and his hair was coiled and springy. "She used to like magic a lot," he told me.

"Well, I don't any more!" Mindy said.

"I don't know what's got into her."

The fezzes were at long last gone and here came another high school band. Everybody clapped and waved. But then there must have been a hitch of some kind, somewhere up front. They came to a halt, still playing, then finished their tune and fell silent and stood staring straight ahead. You could see the little pulses in their temples. You could see the silver chain linking a musician to his piccolo, giving me a sudden comical picture of the accident that must once have happened to make them think of this precaution. I laughed—the loudest sound on the street. For the clapping had stopped by now. There was some understanding between players and audience: each pretended the other wasn't there. Till finally the parade resumed and so did the clapping, and the audience was filled with admiration all over again as if by appointment. The players marched on. Their legs flashed as steadily and evenly as scissors. I was sorry not to have them to watch any more.

"I would think a drum would be a right good instrument," Jake told me, gazing after them.

"You just like whatever booms and damages," said Mindy.

We looked at her.

"Oh! I was going to do my billfold trick," Jake said.

"No, thank you."

"Now, where's my . . . shoot, my billfold."

"Never mind," said Mindy.

"Lend me your billfold, Charlotte," Jake said.

I pulled it out of my purse and gave it to him, meanwhile watching a floatful of white-wigged men signing a paper that was scorched around the edges. "Look close, now," Jake said to Mindy. "Maybe you'll figure how I do it, finally. Here we have a empty billfold, see? Observe there ain't no tricks to this, no hidden pockets, secret compartments . . ." I heard him riffling through it, flicking the plastic windows, snapping up some flap. There was a sudden silence.

"Why," he said. "Why, what have we here. Charlotte? Charlotte, what *is* this?"

I took my eyes away from the parade and looked at what he held out. "It's a traveler's check," I told him.

"A traveler's check! Looky there, Mindy, a hundred-dollar traveler's check! We're rich! Why didn't you tell me?" he asked. "What kind of sneaky way is that to act?"

"I don't know. I didn't think," I said.

"Didn't think? Carrying around a hundred dollars and didn't *think?*"

"Well, I've had it for so long, you see. I mean I had it for just one purpose, I forgot it could be used for anything else."

"What in hell purpose was that?" Jake asked.

"Why, for traveling," I said.

"Charlotte," Jake told me, "we *are* traveling."

"Oh," I said.

12

When Selinda was little, I tried to tell her the truth as much as possible. I told her that as far as I knew, when people die they die and that's the end of it. But after church one day she asked, "How come you and me just die and other people get to go to heaven?"

"Well, there you are," I told her. "You can take your choice."

Selinda chose heaven. I didn't blame her. She went to all those extras that I stayed home from: prayer meetings, Family Night, and so forth. I began to notice her absence. She was seven now and a whole separate person. Well, she always had been, really, but I thought cf seven as the age when people come into their full identity. Sometimes it seemed to me that my own seven-year-old self was still looking out of its grownup hull, wary but unblinking. I asked Selinda, "Will you remember to pay me a visit now and then?"

"I live here," Selinda said.

"Oh, I forgot."

Up till then, I'd thought it would be a mistake to have another child. (More to take with me when I left.) But I changed my mind. And Saul, of course, had wanted more all along. So in January of 1969 I got pregnant. By March I was buying stacks of diapers and flannel nightgowns. In April I had a miscarriage. The doctor said it wouldn't be wise for us to try again.

Nobody knew how much I'd already loved that baby. Not even Mama, who after all had never been consciously pregnant herself. She fussed around with my pillows, looking hopeful and puzzled. Miss Feather brought lots of fluids as if she thought I had a cold. Linus and Selinda acted scared of me; Julian suffered one of his lapses and lost three hundred dollars at the Bowie Racetrack. And Saul sat beside my bed, flattening my hands between his own. He looked not at me but at my fingernails, which had a bluish tinge. He didn't say a word for hours. Wasn't he supposed to? Wasn't it a preacher's job? I said, "Please don't tell me this was God's will."

"I wasn't going to," he said.

I said, "Oh." I felt disappointed. "Because it's not," I said. "It's biological."

"All right."

"This is just something my body did."

"All right."

I studied his face. I saw that he had two sharp lines pulling down the corners of his mouth, so deep they must have been there a long time. His hair was getting thin on top and sometimes now he wore reading glasses. He was thirty-two years old, but looked more like forty-five. I didn't know why. Was it me? I started crying. I said, "Saul, do you think my body did this on purpose?"

"I don't understand."

"Because a baby would have kept me from leaving?"

"Leaving," said Saul.

"Leaving *you.*"

"No, of course not."

"But I just keep thinking, you see. I'm so afraid that . . . I mean, sometimes it seems that we strain at each other so. We're always tugging and chafing and . . . sometimes when we're in the pickup, that rusty, creaky pickup, and Mama's taking two thirds of the seat and Selinda's irking my lap, and I am nagging over something I don't even care about, as if I just want to see how far I can push you, and you've grown disgusted and backed off somewhere in your mind—well, then I think, 'Really, we're a very unhappy family. I don't know why it should come as any surprise,' I think. 'It feels so natural. It's my luck, I'm unlucky, I've lived in unhappy families all my life. I never really expected anything different.' "

I waited to see if Saul would argue, but he didn't. He went on flattening my hands. He kept his head bowed. Already I was sorry I had said it all, but that's the way my life was: I was eternally wishing to take everything back and start over. It was hopeless. I went on.

"Well," I said, "I'm worried that my body thought, 'Now, we don't want to drag this thing out. We surely don't want a *baby;* a baby would stop her from leaving for another whole seven years. So what we should do is just—' "

"Charlotte, you would never leave me," Saul said.

"Listen a minute. I have this check, these shoes, I—"

"But you love me," Saul said. "I know you do."

I looked over at him, his long, steady eyes and set mouth. Why did he always put it that way? That time at the Blue Moon Motel, too. Shouldn't he be telling me how *he* loved *me?*

But what he said was, "I am certain that you care for me, Charlotte."

And another thing: how come it always worked?

I'd been back on my feet six weeks or so when Saul walked into the kitchen one noontime carrying a baby and a blue vinyl diaper bag. Just that suddenly. This was a *large* baby, several months old. A pie-faced, stocky boy baby, looking very stern. "Here," Saul said, and held him out.

"What's that?" I asked, not taking him.

"A baby, of course."

"I'm not supposed to carry heavy things," I said, but I didn't move away. Saul shifted the baby a little higher on his shoulder. He loved children but had never got the knack of holding them right; the baby's nightgown was rucked up to his armpits and he tilted awkwardly, frowning beneath his spikes of hair like a fat blond Napoleon. "Can't you take him? He's not *that* heavy," Saul said.

"But I . . . my hands are cold."

"Guess what, Charlotte? We're going to keep him a while."

"Ah, Saul," I said. You think I wasn't expecting that? Nothing could surprise me any more. In this impermanent state of mine, events drifted in like passing seaweed and brushed my cheek and drifted out again. I saw them clearly from a great distance, both coming and going. "Thank you for the thought," I said, "but it wouldn't be possible," and I moved on around the table, serenely setting out soupbowls.

"Charlotte, he hasn't got a father, his mother ran off and left him with his grandmother, and this morning we found the grandmother dead. I assumed you'd want him."

"But then his mother will come back," I said. "We could lose him at any moment." I started folding napkins.

"We could lose anybody at any moment. We could lose Selinda."

"You know what I mean," I said. "He isn't ours."

"Nobody's ours," said Saul.

So I finished folding the last of the napkins, and warmed my hands in my apron a minute, and came back to where Saul was standing. There was some comfort in knowing I had no choice. Everything had been settled for me. Even the baby seemed to see that, and leaned forward as if he'd expected me all along and dropped like a stone into my waiting arms.

We called him Jiggs. His real name was something poor-white that I tried not ever to think about, and Jiggs seemed better suited anyway to his stubby shape and the thick, clear-rimmed spectacles that he very soon had to start wearing. Also, Jiggs was such an offhand name. I might as easily have called him Butch, or Buster or Punkin or Pee Wee. Anything that showed how lightly I would give him back when his mother came to claim him.

We sat him in a pile of blocks in my studio whenever I was working. Linus built him teetering cities, Selinda drew crayon horses for him to ponder. I would talk to him continuously as I moved the lamps around. "Is he yours?" a customer might ask, and I would say, "Oh no, that's Jiggs."

"Ah."

And I would photograph their polite, baffled faces.

For I was still taking pictures, but just because people happened to stop by. And only on a day-to-day basis. And I had lost, somewhere along the line, my father's formal composition. During the years stray props had moved it: flowers, swords, Ping-Pong paddles, overflow from Alberta's clutter. People had a way of picking up odd objects when they entered, and then they got attached to them. They would sit down still holding them, absent-mindedly, and half the time I never even noticed. I wasn't a chatty, *personal* kind of photographer. I would be occupied judging the light, struggling with the camera that had grown more crotchety than ever. Its bellows were all patched with little squares of electrical tape. Its cloth was so frayed and dusty I got sneezing fits. Often I would have gone as far as printing up a negative before I really saw what I had taken. "Why," I would say to Linus. "What on earth . . . ?"

Then Linus would set the baby aside and the two of us would study my photo: some high school girl in Alberta's sequined shawl, strung with loops of curtain-beads, holding a plume of peacock feathers and giving us a dazed, proud, beautiful smile, as if she knew how she had managed to astonish us.

In the fall of 1972, Alberta died. We got a telegram from her father-in-law. YOUR MOTHER DEAD OF HEART FAILURE FUNERAL 10 A.M. WEDNESDAY. When he read it, Saul turned grim but said nothing. Later he called Linus and Julian into the sunporch and they held a conference with the doors closed. I hung around outside, fiddling with strands of my hair. When it came to matters of importance, I thought, I was not remotely a part of that family. Here I assumed I had broken into their circle, found myself some niche in the shelter of Alberta's shadow, but it turned out the Emorys were as shut away as ever and Alberta had gone and died. Underneath I had always expected her back, I believe. I wanted her approval; she was so much braver, freer, stronger than I had turned out to be. There were a thousand things I had planned on holding up for her to pass judgment on. Now it seemed that these things had no point any more, and I thought of them all—even the children—with a certain flat dislike.

I went to find my mother, who was knitting in front of the TV. "Alberta has died," I told her.

"Oh, my soul," said Mama, not missing a stitch. But then she never had thought much of her. "Well, I suppose the men will be going to the funeral."

But they didn't, as it happened. That was the subject of

the conference. Saul had told them *he* wasn't going, and he
didn't think they should either, but that was up to them. They
discussed it carefully, examining all the issues. This was what
they'd come to: her gloriously wicked sons, now aging and
balding and troubled by pathetic, minor errors. In her absence,
their colors had faded. People are only reflections in other people's eyes, it turns out. In Alberta's absence her house had
crumbled and vanished, her belongings had taken on a rusty
smell. (She told me once that the Emorys had always been
killed by horses; that was their mode of dying. But in her absence it emerged that only one had been: a distant uncle. The
others had passed away in their beds, puny deaths they would
have been spared if Alberta had only stayed around.)

Julian said he wouldn't attend the funeral either. That left
Linus, the only one who might have liked to go, but everybody
knew that he wouldn't defy his brothers. (Linus had a beard
because he never had shaved, not ever, since the day his first
whiskers grew in. That was how little he fought things.) "I'll
just stay at home and say a prayer for her in my mind," he told
Saul.

"Whatever you like," Saul said.

It was Linus I heard this from, of course. Never Saul.
Linus sat on a kitchen chair later, sanding a piece of wood the
size of a postage stamp. For a couple of years now, he had been
building dollhouse furniture. I don't know why. And all of a
sudden he said to me, "In my opinion, he should forgive her."

"What?"

"Saul," said Linus, "should forgive our mother."

"Oh well, let him have *one* sin."

"On the sunporch he said, 'What makes me laugh is, that
crazy old man outlived her after all.' Grandpa, he meant. Then
he really did laugh. Threw back his head and laughed out loud.
What do you make of that?"

"Nothing," I said. "I don't even try. Leave him alone."

So Linus blew a speck of sawdust away, and wiped his forehead with one veiny brown arm and fell silent. He was used to my protecting *him,* not Saul. He didn't guess how often I had asked myself the same question: What do you make of Saul?

Saul had become a man of blacks and whites. In the pulpit, looming black robe with a wide white neckband; the rest of the time, cheap black suit and white shirt. Often, while buying groceries or walking with the children, I would catch sight of him striding through the town on some wild mission—larger than life, with his unbuttoned suit coat billowing out behind him, trouser cuffs flapping, tie fluttering, strings of neglected hair feathering over his collar. He carried a Bible, always, and wore a dark, intense expression, as if narrowing in on something. Most of the time, he didn't even see us.

Was he just a fanatical preacher, bent on converting the world?

But sometimes when giving his sermons he stumbled and halted, and appeared to be considering the words he had just spoken. Then I would have to consider them myself, trying to discover what truth might lie within them. Sometimes, while lashing out against the same old evils, he would stop in midsentence and sag and shake his head and walk away, forgetting to say the benediction. Then his bewildered, ever smaller flock would rustle in their pews, and I would sit gripping my gloves. Should I run after him? Should I let him be? I pictured some great substructure shifting and creaking inside him. I felt my own jagged edges grinding together as they settled into new positions. At night, I often woke with a start and pressed my face against his damp, matted chest. Even his heartbeat seemed muffled and secret. I never was able to imagine what he dreamed.

I was moving around the kitchen one day in the spring of 1974, serving up breakfast to a man from the mourners' bench.

Dr. Sisk. I was trying to hurry Jiggs along because it was nearly time for kindergarten and he was just sitting there with one sock on and nothing else. I was tripping over the dog, this terrible dog that Selinda had brought home from Girl Scouts. It wasn't one of my quieter times, in other words. So it took me a minute to notice what I assumed to be Saul from another age, leaning in the doorway—the Saul I married, with a calmer face and no lines around his mouth, a little more hair on top, easier and looser and less preoccupied. He wore faded, tattered jeans and carried an Army surplus knapsack. He watched me with a kind of wry amusement that Saul had long ago lost. Well, I wasn't so very surprised. In fact I'd already thought of an explanation for it (some simple time warp, nothing to get alarmed about) when he spoke. "I knocked but nobody answered," he said.

It wasn't Saul's voice at all, and never had been; didn't have that echo behind it. I said, "Amos!"

"How you doing, Charlotte?"

He straightened up and came to offer me his hand. By now I was so used to various people wandering in it didn't occur to me to ask why he was here. (I'd been expecting him for years, to tell the truth. Wondered what was keeping him.) But Amos seemed to think he had to tell me. "Hear Clarion High School is looking for a music teacher," he said. "I thought I might apply. I guess I should've dropped a line ahead of time but I'm not too much of a letter writer."

He had sent us fifteen letters in all the time we'd been married—if you count a Hallmark wedding card and about fourteen of those printed change-of-address notices that you pick up free from the post office. But that's the way the Emorys did things. I said, "Never mind, have some breakfast. Meet Jiggs and Dr. Sisk."

Jiggs stood up in his one striped sock and shook hands. He was always a dignified child, even naked, and looked like a kindly little old man in his stodgy glasses. I was proud to show him off. But Amos gave him a puzzled stare and said, "Jiggs?"

Then Dr. Sisk rose too, jarring the table, and leaned across the scrambled eggs to offer one freckled, webby hand. "Arthur Sisk," he said. "From the mourners' bench."

"Mourners' bench," said Amos, still waiting.

"I was contemplating suicide. Preacher up and offered me an alternative solution."

"Have some more eggs," I told Dr. Sisk.

"No thank you, darlin', maybe later," he said. He turned back to Amos. "Life was getting me down. Grinding on so. The tedium! I'm a G.P. All those infants with upper respiratory infections, Vicks VapoRub smeared on their chests. Stethoscope goes 'Sppk!' when you pull it away. I thought of suicide."

"Is that so," said Amos.

"Preacher talked me out of it. Recommended I give my life to Christ, instead. Well, I liked the way he put it. I mean, just to hand my life *over.* Isn't that true, my dear," he said to me.

"Well," I said, "but you still have income tax and license renewals."

"Beg pardon?"

"Still have bank statements and dental appointments and erroneous bills," I said. "If it were all that easy, don't you think I'd long ago have handed *my* life over?"

Dr. Sisk sat down and started pulling at his nose.

"Help yourself to some eggs," I told Amos.

"What?" Amos said. "Oh . . . no, really I . . ."

"Saul is paying a hospital visit, he ought to be back before long."

"Well, do . . . I mean, funny, I thought it was a daughter you had," Amos said. He took a handful of his hair. "Didn't you send me a birth announcement? Daughter named Catherine."

"Oh yes, that would be Selinda," I said. "She's already left for school."

"Selinda."

"This is Jiggs."

"I see. Jiggs," said Amos. He let go of his hair but continued looking confused.

Then Jiggs seemed to feel he had to stand up all over again, flashing white moons off his fingerprinted spectacles. "Jiggs, *please*," I said. "In fifteen minutes you have to be ready to leave. Would you like some coffee, Amos?"

"No, thanks, I stopped for breakfast in Holgate."

"Well, come and sit in the living room," I said, and I led him down the hall, untying my apron as I went. "I hope you don't mind the mess. It's still a little early in the day."

There *was* a mess, but nothing that would clear up as the day went on. Some guests can make you see these things. I had never realized, for instance, how very much dollhouse furniture Linus had produced in the last few years. People kept offering to buy it from him for fabulous amounts, but he wouldn't sell. It was all for me, he said. Now on every tabletop there were other tables, two inches high. Also breakfronts, cupboards, and bureaus, as well as couches upholstered in velvet and dining room chairs with needlepoint seats. And each tiny surface bore its own accessories: lamps with toothpaste-cap shades, books made from snippets of magazine bindings, and single wooden beads containing arrangements of dried baby's breath. Entire roomfuls were grouped beneath the desk and under the piano. I could see that Amos was startled. "They're Linus's," I told him. "He makes them."

"*Oh*, yes," said Amos. He sat down on the couch, letting his moccasins sprawl out across the rug. "How is Linus these days?"

"He's fine."

"No more of his . . . trouble?"

"Oh no, he seems very steady. Right now he's over at the laundromat with Mama."

"And is Julian in these parts?"

"He's down at the shop already," I said.

"What shop?"

"The radio shop."

"*Dad's* radio shop?"

"Well, where have you been?" I asked. "Doesn't Saul keep in touch?"

"At Christmas he just sends this card from the church," said Amos, "telling me to bear in mind the true meaning."

"Oh, I see," I said. "Well, Julian works at the radio shop. It's TV now, mostly, but we still *call* it the radio shop. He's doing just fine. I really believe his lapses are going to get fewer."

"Is that right," said Amos. He drummed his fingers on his knapsack.

"Pretty soon we'll start trusting him with money again, but meanwhile the customers just come by here and pay Miss Feather instead."

"Miss . . . ?"

"But what about you?" I asked. "Do you think you'll get this job?"

"Oh, sure, the principal wrote and told me it's mine if I want it. And I guess I do want it. I've been in one place too long; it's time for a change. And I'd just broken off with this girl, felt ready to . . . though I'm not so certain that I could take Clarion again. I wish this offer had turned up someplace else."

"There's nothing wrong with Clarion," I said. (I don't know why.)

"No, of course not, it's fine," said Amos. "I didn't mean it wasn't."

He hooked his thumbs in his belt and tipped his head back against the couch, closing the conversation. I remembered that

Amos used to be the Emory who ran away. Maybe he still was. Weaknesses came one to a person in that family, and could be conquered but not destroyed; they merely moved on to someone else. To Julian. Julian was collecting weaknesses like so many coins or postage stamps. Saul's old trouble with girls was Julian's now and so was Linus's tendency to break down. We all loved Julian a lot, and no wonder. We were fond of his smudgy, weary eyes and exhausted good looks, and if he took on Amos's habit of running away then we would be in trouble. I said, "Amos, do you still run away?"

He seemed to have been caught off-guard. "What?" he said. "Well, no, for heaven's sake, why would you ask a thing like that? Of course not."

"Where did it go?" I asked him.

"What?"

But before I could explain, in came Saul, stooping automatically in the doorway. He stopped. "Amos?" he said.

Amos stood up and said, "Hello, Saul."

"We've waited a long time for you," Saul told him, and set a hand on his shoulder. I was smiling as I watched, but what I wondered was: why did Amos look so much younger, when he was the oldest of the Emory boys?

Now they were complete, the four of them under one roof again. Amos's job didn't start till fall, so meanwhile he helped at the radio shop. Also, he got our old piano tuned and practiced every day. It never failed to amaze me that Amos had become a musician. Having barely scraped through school, he'd fallen into music like a duck finally hitting water and worked his way gladly through the Peabody Institute. Amos Emory! He sat hunched at the yellow-toothed piano playing Chopin, his moccasins set gingerly among the dollhouse furniture, elbows close to his sides as if he feared to damage the keys with his huge square hands. A rag of black hair fell over his forehead. "This has got to be the worst piano I've ever come across," he told me, but he continued pulling in its faded, tinny, long-ago notes.

Unfortunately, I don't like piano. Something about it has always irritated me. But Mama loved to hear him; she'd been musical herself once, she said. And Selinda often paused on her way to someplace else and listened from the door. She was thirteen that summer and had suddenly turned beautiful. Her hair was blonder from the sun and she had these burnished, threadlike eyebrows and dusty freckles. And close behind her you'd generally find Jiggs, who came running from anywhere as soon as he heard music. He coaxed lessons from Amos and then practiced what he learned for hours at a time—plodding about on the keys, breathing through his mouth, fogging up his spectacles. Whenever I passed through the living room, I would smile at the back of his soft fair head and make my eternal, evil wish: Please let his mother drop dead somewhere, I'll never hope for anything else in my life.

At dinner I could look down a straight row of Emory boys (skipping Dr. Sisk, who poked in everywhere) and see four variations on a single theme—all those large, sober faces, Saul in black, Julian in a flashy turtleneck, Linus wearing something limp and unnoticeable and Amos in tatters of denim, like an easygoing, good-natured hitch-hiker. Well, he was easygoing. He was good-natured. Then why did he get on my nerves so?

He was always asking me questions. What I thought of Holy Basis; why we had so much furniture; how I could stand so many strangers coming through. "What strangers?" I said.

"Oh, Miss Feather, Dr. Sisk . . ."

"Miss Feather's been with us near as long as Selinda. I wouldn't really call her a stranger."

"And what causes Saul to look the way he does?"

"I don't know what you're talking about," I said.

"He's got so . . . shadowed, he's got this haunted look. Is everything all right?"

"Of course it's all right, don't be silly," I said.

He studied the ceiling a while. "I don't suppose it's easy, being a preacher's wife," he said.

"Why would you think that?"

"Well, having him so, well, saintly. Right?"

I stared straight through him.

"Or for him, either; it wouldn't be easy married to *you*. Selinda says you aren't religious. Doesn't that scare him?"

"Scare him? It makes him angry," I said.

"It scares him. Of course it does, the way you coast along, no faith, all capability, your . . . *sparseness*, and you're the one that makes the soup while he just brings home the sinners to eat it. Isn't that so? He forever has to keep wrestling with the thoughts that you put in his mind."

"I don't! I never *touch* his mind! I deliberately keep back from it," I said.

"He wrestles anyway," said Amos. He grinned. "His private devil." Then he grew serious. He said, "I don't understand married people."

"Evidently not," I told him, stiffly.

"How they can keep on keeping together. Though it's admirable, of course."

What he meant was, it might be admirable but *he* didn't admire it. Well, I didn't admire him, either. I disliked the careless way he moved around the room, examining various cabinets no bigger than matchboxes. Faced with Amos's scorn, I underwent some subtle change; I grew loyal, stubborn. I forgot the plans for my trip, I reflected that it would be pointless: no matter where I went, Saul would be striding forever down the alleys of my mind, slapping his Bible against his thigh. "You don't know the first thing about it," I told Amos.

But Amos just said, "No, probably I don't," and went on easily to something new. "Whose dog is that?"

"Selinda's."

"*Peculiar* kind of animal."

Well, it's true that Ernest wasn't worth much. He was a mongrel—a huge black beast, going gray, with long tangled hair and a mop-shaped head. When Ernest wagged his tail, everything at his end of the room fell and broke. Some form of hearing loss led him to believe that we were calling him whenever we called Amos or Linus, and he always arrived drooling and panting, withering us with his fish-market breath, skidding and crashing into things and scraping the floor with his toenails. Also, he'd become unduly attached to me and any time I left him alone he lost control of his bladder. Oh, I admit he wasn't perfect.

Still, I didn't see what business it was of Amos's. "Tell me," I said, "is there one single thing here you approve of? Shall we throw the whole place out and start over?"

Then Amos held up one hand, backing off, and said, "All right, all right, don't take it wrong." He was smiling his shy, sweet, hitch-hiker's smile, lowering his head, looking out from under his shaggy eyebrows. Instantly I felt sorry for him. He was just new here, that was all. He had left home longer ago than his brothers, traveled farther, forgotten more. Forgotten that in every family there are certain ways you shrink and stretch to accommodate other people. Why, Linus for instance could remember back to his nursing days (Alberta's nipple like a mouthful of crumpled seersucker, he claimed) but Amos couldn't stand to remember and told me so, outright. He hadn't liked being a child, he said. Their mother had been pushy, clamorous, violent, taking over their lives, meddling in their brains, demanding a constant torrent of admiration and gaiety. Her sons had winced when she burst into their rooms. She breathed her hot breath on them, she laughed her harsh laugh.

She called for parties! dancing! let's show a little *life* here!
Given anything less than what she needed, he said (and she
was always given less, she could never get enough), she turned
mocking and contemptuous. She had a tongue like a knife. The
sharp, insistent colors of her clothes and even of her skin, her
hair, were painful to her children's eyes. They had hated her.
They had wished her dead.

Alberta?

"Why are you surprised?" Amos asked me. "Do we look
like four normal, happy men? Hasn't it occurred to you? The
other three can't even seem to leave Clarion; and I'm not much
better, hopping around like something in a skillet, running before the school year's even finished half the time and breaking
with whoever gets close to me. Three of us have never married;
the fourth chose somebody guaranteed to let him keep his
doors shut."

I stared at him.

"Isn't it true? You don't know a thought in his head,
never asked. If you had, none of this would come as any surprise to you. Saul hates Alberta worse than any of us."

"But . . . no, that's only because of . . ."

I didn't want to come right out and say it.

"Because of Grandpa?" Amos asked. "Face it: single
events don't cause that kind of effect. It took Saul years and
years to get as bitter as he is. He's come away from her in
shreds; all of us have. He and the others just sit here in Clarion
circling her grave and picking at her bones, trying to sort it
through, but not me. I gave up. I don't remember. I've forgotten."

And he did, in fact, smile at me with the clear, blank eyes
of a man without a past. I could tell he had truly forgotten. He
had twisted every bit of it, muddled his facts hopelessly. There
was no point in trying to set him straight.

I took him with us to church. He sat beside me, dressed in

a borrowed suit, scrubbed and subdued. But even here, he seemed to be asking his questions. The moment Saul announced his text—Matthew 12:30, "He that is not with me is against me"—Amos shifted his feet, as if about to lean forward and shoot up a hand and shout, "Objection!" But he didn't, of course. It was all in my mind. He sat there as quiet as anyone, with his fingers laced. I don't know how he managed to annoy me so.

That night I dreamed that Saul and I had found ourselves a bedroom of a watery green color, like an aquarium. We were making love under flickering shadows, and for once there was no tiny knock on our door, no sad little voice: "I'm lonesome," no church members phoning with deaths and diseases. Saul looked down at my face with a peculiarly focused, thoughtful look, as if he had some plan in mind for me. I decided the new bedroom was a wonderful idea. Then Linus stretched out alongside me and covered me with soft, bearded kisses, and Julian arrived in his gambling clothes which he slowly took off, one by one, smiling at me all the while. I was circled by love, protected on every side. The only Emory who wasn't there was Amos, and he was who they were protecting me from.

13

The sign said: PERTH MANOR MOTEL. $8 NITELY. ANTIQUES. ATTIC TREASURES. NOTARY PUBLIC. PUREBRED DALMATIONS. We paused on the sidewalk to read it. Twilight had slipped in more suddenly than usual, it seemed to me. We'd been taken by surprise, had our eyes clapped over by some cool-handed stranger coming up behind us. But this sign was written in movable white letters such as you see in cafeterias where the menu often changes, and we could easily make it out. Behind it was a small plain building, mostly porch, with OFFICE glowing on one pillar. Further back we saw a string of cottages no bigger then henhouses, the faded color of something chalked up and then rubbed away.

"Now first," said Jake, "we check that Oliver's mom is not around."

"What for?" Mindy asked.

"Oliver's mom don't think too highly of me."

"Then why are we coming here, Jake?"

"Well, I have some hopes of Oliver," he said.

My loafers gritted on the sidewalk; so did Mindy's sandals. Jake gave us an exasperated look and motioned for us to stop. He went on up the walk alone in his sneakers. We stayed where we were, eerily still in the gathering dusk, Mindy like a weightless, glowing balloon. I was either tired or hungry (too numb to know which) and had reached that state where nothing seems real. Mindy's pale hand pressed to her backache could have been my own. I held my breath along with Jake when he crept up the steps to peer through the screen.

"He is going to get himself caught," Mindy said.

Jake swatted an arm backwards in her direction, warning her to be still.

"Sometimes he just *tempts* people to catch him. Watch," she said.

But no, here he came, shaking his head, extra bouncy on his heels from having had to hold still so long. "It's Mrs. Jamison, sure enough," he told us. "Potato on toothpicks, standing at the counter, hoping for someone to look down on."

"Maybe she won't know who you are," Mindy said.

"Are you kidding? Every night she prays I fall out of a window," said Jake. "We'll just sit here a while."

He was talking about a slatted bench that stood at the edge of the yard, facing the street. We sat down on it, Mindy in the middle. It was one of those lukewarm, breezy evenings that make you feel you're expecting something. We sat like people in a movie house, but all we had to watch was a dingy men's store across the way and a few passing cars. Periodically Jake would crane around toward the office door—a narrow rectangle full of light.

"What if she's there for the evening?" Mindy asked him.

"We stay somewheres else and come back the next day. Rent us a room with Charlotte's traveler's check."

"Oh, Jake, I'm beat. Can't we just go on in and pay no mind what she says to you?"

"I wouldn't face that woman for nothing," Jake said. "I'm scared to death of her."

I thought that was funny. I started laughing, but stopped when he glared at me. "Why don't you just shove a pistol in her ribs?" I said.

Oh, I was even tireder than I'd thought. Jake drew his head in sharply. Mindy said, "Pistol?"

"Lady's crazy," he told her. He had his arm along the back of the seat, and now he started stroking her shoulder like someone calming a cat. "Fact is, Oliver's mom has always disliked me," he said. "I believe she ties me up in her mind with things I never had no part in. Various misfortunes of Oliver's. It wasn't me put those bombs in no mailboxes, I didn't even know him then. Didn't know him till training school. But try and tell *her* that. She sees me, she thinks 'Trouble'."

"She's not the only one," Mindy said.

Their voices had taken on that clear, anonymous sound that comes at twilight. They might have been campers telling ghost stories, strollers talking under someone's window, parents heard from far across a lawn.

"When the two of us got out of training school," Jake said, "why, I would drop over to see him sometimes. He didn't live all that much of a distance. He lived with his mom, who was a real estate lady. I would find him home reading, all he done was reading. We'd ride around, go out for a hamburger, you know how it is. I really had a good time with that Oliver. But only if his mom wasn't there. His mom was so brisky and dry of voice. Never smiled unless she was saying something mean. Like she'd say, 'Back so soon, Jack?' She always called me Jack, which is definitely not my name. That can grate on a person. 'Funny,' she'd say, 'I thought you were here just yesterday. No doubt I was mistaken.' With this small sweet smile

curling up her mouth while she was talking. I hate a woman to
do that."

"That's how *my* mother did you," said Mindy. "You just
have this knack, I believe." She told me, "My mother used to
be so rude to him! Now she pretends he's not alive and never
will mention his name. I ask in my letters if she's seen him and
all she'll answer back is how many inches of rain they've had.
He could fall down dead and *she* wouldn't tell me. To her he's
dead already."

"Well, that explains it," Jake said.

"What's it explain?"

"Anyway," said Jake, "you may laugh that I'd let Mrs.
Jamison get to me but I couldn't help it. I mean I just couldn't
help it. See, at the time my own mom was right disappointed in
me too though nowhere near as mean, of course. She would
just act pale and slumpy and bow her head real low over her
sewing. Know how they do? I went to Oliver's to get away from
her, but met up then with Oliver's mom. Seems I had been
characterized as someone no-account. Seems I couldn't shake
other people's picture of me."

I gave a sudden sigh. Mindy crossed her ankles, and her
dress stirred and whispered.

"Well, I run off," said Jake. "I heard of this guy that
would pay you for driving a car to California. I just wanted to
get gone and so I left with no goodbyes. Not that I kept it a
secret on purpose, but my mom happened to be visiting a lady
down the street when I received word and what I thought was,
'I've got to get *free!* Got to go, can't stay here no more.' Only
they arrested me in California for running a stolen automobile.
Well, I didn't draw a sentence or nothing. It was all cleared up.
But things were a little complicated on account of past troubles
I'd had, and time I got home it was some months later and
Oliver'd gone to Florida. I asked his neighbors. 'Why, him and
his mother packed up some weeks ago and moved to Perth,

Florida, where it's less crime she says and a better class of people, and the sun shines so steady there they give you your newspaper free on any day it rains.' And sure enough, that Christmas and every Christmas after I would get a card from O.J., Florida-type, Santa Claus riding a surfboard, angels picking grapefruit. 'Merry Christmas, Jake, I hope you're well.' And I would put some effort into answering, though let me tell you I'm not what you'd call a letter writer. Talk about all I was doing and all, spend quite some time on it. But the only thing *he* ever sent was those Christmas cards. Only Christmas cards. Made me feel like he was in jail, you know? Just that one card a year, maybe censored; surprised if she didn't check my letters for hacksaws and razor blades. Well, I blame myself, really. I never should have left him with his mom like that. Why didn't I drop around his house before I run, ask him to come on along? But I was just so anxious to get going, you see. Just so desperate to leave."

We watched a stream of cars flow past us, colorless in the twilight, packed with wan, exhausted faces straining southward.

"The trouble is," said Jake, "when people are thinking ill of you you just have this urge to get out, you know? You say, now if I could just gather myself together again. If I could just start my life over somehow."

"That's true," I said.

"I really believe," he told me, "that any time you see someone running, it's their old, faulty self they're running from. Or other people's *notion* of their faulty self. But I don't know, I don't know."

Then he stood up, took a few steps onto the grass, and leaned toward the door of the office. "She's gone," he said.

"Who's there now?" Mindy asked.

"Nobody, looks like."

He stood waiting, with his back to us. Mindy set her skirt

out all around her. "Notice he hasn't even *mentioned* supper," she told me. "Thoughtless? And I got low blood sugar."

"Hot dog! Here comes some other guy," said Jake. "We can ask him. Let's go, ladies."

We rose disjointedly and followed him. Up the walk, up the steps, across the creaky porch. Through the orange glow of the overhead light—bugproof, supposedly, but that didn't stop a whole herd of brown moths from puttering about near my hair.

Though it wasn't fully dark outside yet, we had to blink when we stepped in the door. Yellow lamps lit the room, glaring off the cracked linoleum. Behind a counter cluttered with ashtrays, magazines, and sightseeing brochures, a lanky, sand-colored man with floppy blond hair stood rubber-stamping envelopes. He didn't look up when we came in. He kept his head bent, his bony hand pacing steadily between envelopes and stamp pad as if he took real pleasure in the rhythm. "Be with you in a minute," was all he said, in a deep, cracked voice that seemed younger than he did.

"Well, I'm hunting Oliver Jamison," said Jake. "You know him?"

Then the man stopped working and looked up. His eyes were not so much blue as transparent, but they darkened while I watched. "Why, Jake," he said.

"Huh?"

"You don't recognize me."

"Oliver?"

Neither of them seemed happy to meet. Jake had a stunned, uncertain expression; Oliver looked concerned. He said, "You shouldn't be around here, Jake."

"Why not?"

"Don't you know the cops are hunting you?"

Mindy clapped a hand to her mouth. From somewhere to the rear, a woman called, "Who is it, Ollie?"

"No one, Ma."

He set down his stamp and came around the counter. "Let's go outdoors," he told us. Up close I saw the white squint lines breaking up his tan, I smelled the clean smell of his pale plaid shirt. He was one of those ambling, gentle-faced men who never act startled. He seemed like somebody I might know. Or maybe it was this place we were in—clearly a home, in spite of the counter, with a tangle of baby-blue knitting abandoned in an armchair. I felt suddenly disoriented. I stumbled after him, nudged by Jake, out the door and down the porch steps, deep enough into the yard so that we could be hidden by twilight. Then we stopped. Mindy reached out and touched one finger to Oliver's forearm. "Why would they be after him?" she asked. "Is it on account of me? He hasn't done wrong."

"Is that true?" Oliver said. He turned to Jake. "They came by yesterday. They got my name from your address book. It was the only one in there besides the liquor store, they said, and so they tracked me down, wondered if I'd seen you. I said no. And Ma did too, of course, and Claire had no idea who they meant."

"Who's Claire?" Jake asked.

"My wife."

"Wife?"

"They told me you had pulled this crazy . . . but you didn't, did you?"

"Well, I don't know. Sort of," said Jake. He jammed his hands in his pockets and gazed off across the street.

"But . . . I mean, it doesn't sound logical. Had something gone wrong? What would make you hit that fool bank for that piddling amount? And hostage! Taking a . . . and now who've you got? Who's a hostage here and who isn't?" he asked.

Mindy said, "Hostage?"

He focused on me. "Lord, Jake," he said.

I felt that I was shriveling up.

"But Oliver," said Jake, "just let me tell you. This wasn't nothing I planned, you know. Seems like things just worked out this way. I'm a victim of impulse, right? Look, now, you're the one last hope I have. You're the last way open to me. Oliver? O.J.? Can't you just give us a room to stay the night in? Sit down with me and figure some way out of this, Oliver. I'm just not *up* to handling things on my own right now. It's all started getting muddled."

"I'm sorry," Oliver said. "I'd like to help. But Ma would call the police, you know she would. It's not her fault; she's old and she's scared and she still isn't over that mailbox business. And Claire, well, she's having a difficult pregnancy and I don't want her getting upset. You see my position?"

"Yeah, well. Sure," Jake said.

"Jake, maybe you ought to turn yourself in."

We were very quiet. A woman's voice sailed out across the lawn. "Ollie?"

Jake said, "Your mama's calling."

"Think about it, Jake."

"Why don't you just *go,*" said Jake. "Your mom will be out here in two minutes flat. Just go, why don't you, tend to that little life of yours."

"Jake, I'm twenty-six years old now," said Oliver.

But he didn't get any answer to that. He waited a while, looking toward Jake with some expression that I couldn't make out in the dark. Then he said, "Well. So long, I guess," and walked away. A minute later I heard the screen door shut—a summer evening sound that hung on and on. The three of us stood in the yard, empty-handed. We kept on looking at the rich gold rectangle of the door, even though there was nobody there.

Then Mindy said, "Well, I just don't understand this thing in any manner whatsoever."

"Hush up," said Jake. "Let me think."

He was rubbing his forehead, over and over. His profile was stark and jutting, like something hastily cut from black construction paper. Mindy tipped forward to look at him. "Please, Jake," she said. "Will you please tell me what is going on?"

"Hush *up,* Mindy."

"I've got a right to know."

"Come on, let's get in the car," he said.

He started toward the street. I stayed where I was. Without saying anything, he came back and clamped my arm and led me forward. Mindy followed. She kept saying, "Jake?"

The car listed under a streetlight. I was used to squinting at it in the sun and saw, now, what I had missed before: in the course of our trip we had wrecked it pretty thoroughly. Its rear end was caved in, one tail-light hollow, front bumper gone, and there were long weedy scratches across its side. Jake opened the door to a cavernous blackness, a strong cat smell, a welter of candy wrappers and potato chip bags. A Pepsi can clanged to the pavement and rolled a great distance. I jerked free of Jake's hand and stepped back. "Get in," Jake told me.

I shook my head.

"Please get in, Charlotte."

"No," I said.

"Now listen, there's people walking up, don't make me look bad. You want to complicate things just when I'm feeling so down? Climb on in; act natural."

"Fool! How can she act natural when she's a what's-it, hostage?" Mindy asked him.

But actually, it seemed perfectly natural. I slid along the seat to my old, familiar place. Folded my hands across my purse. Jake arrived next to me, Mindy came last and fitted her stomach behind the steering wheel and closed the door. Well. Here we all were. I had never in my life felt so cramped and poverty-stricken.

"Now, let me think," Jake told us.

"Think about this: I could get arrested for aiding and abetting," said Mindy.

"Will you just let me figure this out?"

"I could have my baby in jail, and all for something I never had the faintest notion of."

"Oh, shoot, Mindy," said Jake, "anybody else would have *guessed*. Why'd you think I had that chain on the door?"

"For a derby, of course! For a demolition derby! You often chain the doors when you're driving a derby."

"Well, this is clearly not no derby," said Jake. He jerked a thumb at the ignition key. "Start her up, please."

"Where we going?"

"Find a place to cash Charlotte's check. Bank that's open Friday evenings."

"But—"

"Do you want my company or don't you?"

Mindy started the car. We pulled out into traffic. Everyone else was driving so wearily and steadily, it was like joining up with a river. "I sure would like to eat," Mindy said.

"We'll do that after," said Jake. He was slumped in his seat, watching passing signs indifferently. "Can you figure it?" he asked me. "Guy like Oliver, used to be so cool, used to read a book in the training school, *read!* like nothing could ever bother him. Oliver, married. Settled. Expecting. Grown so old I didn't know him. But he knew *me*, boy. You don't see *me* all changed about."

"I kind of liked him," I said.

"You would," said Jake. "That poor sucker."

"Well, I didn't think he was so badly off."

"You just say that because you have to," Jake said. He told Mindy, "Charlotte here is married, you know."

"Yes, I know," said Mindy.

"Married to a preacher."

Mindy slowed for a stop sign.

"Isn't that right?" Jake asked me.

I nodded. I was watching a neon martini glass that kept rapidly emptying and refilling.

"She helps in the Sunday School, teaching 'Jesus Loves Me.' Counsels the Youth Fellowship in how to stay out of temptation."

"I do not," I said.

"Her and her husband never ever argue, they just take their troubles to the Lord in prayer."

"Don't be ridiculous, we argue all the time," I said.

"You do?"

"Of course we do."

"What about?"

"None of your business," I said.

It was silly; I was beginning to cry. I had tears in my eyes for no earthly reason. But of course I didn't let Jake see them. I kept on looking out the side window. Crying makes me angry and so I started talking, louder than usual. "We disagree on everything," I said. "He's always finding fault, he says I'm . . . he holds the stupidest things against me. Like, one morning he was going off to Bible College and I said, 'Don't take any wooden nickels.' Well, it was just something to say, I didn't mean anything by it. But he's never forgotten. Fifteen years ago! He imagines all these undercurrents that I had never intended. He had this revivalist speak last summer, it's an annual thing; they set up a tent in the kite field. But Saul came back so moody and quiet, said he hadn't enjoyed it at all, hadn't been able to take it in; he'd continually heard my comments on every word the preacher said. But I wasn't even there! And I would never do that, I really try to keep from . . . but Saul said, 'I heard your voice. Cool, flat voice. No part of that sermon could come through to me. How am I going to handle this?' I've come to stand for everything bad. I think he sees me as evil. I tell him, 'Look, I don't have to belong to Holy Basis to be a good woman. I try my very best,' I say. 'Is it my fault I'm not religious?' I never have been, not since I was seven and they gave me this book of children's Bible stories, this jealous God throwing tantrums, people having to sacrifice their children, everybody always in the wrong. I didn't like it. See, it's not that I don't *believe.* Sometimes I do, sometimes I don't, it depends on when you ask me. What the trouble is: I don't approve. I'd rather not be associated with it. It's against my principles. 'I try to manage without all that,' I say, 'and really, it's harder to be good if you do it without religion. Give me an A for effort at least,' I tell him . . ."

"But then how come he said all that on TV?" Jake asked.

I had trouble breaking off my train of thought. I said, "What?"

"Said you was a good woman."

"Oh . . . did he? I don't know, I guess he just meant I wouldn't have robbed a bank."

"Then why didn't he *say* you wouldn't have robbed a bank?" said Jake. "What his words were, you're a good woman."

I looked at him.

"Maybe he sees things different now you've left," said Jake. "Or more likely, you just had him figured wrong to start with. I mean, it could be he really does believe you're good, and worries what that means for *his* side. Ever thought of that?"

"Well, no," I said.

"Women," said Jake. "They can't understand the very simplest little things."

We rode along in silence, threading down an avenue of lights as blurred and dazzling as a double strand of jewels.

14

One morning in the fall of 1974, I was mixing Jiggs some cocoa and dreaming at the kitchen sink. My mother said, "Charlotte, I don't feel so well," and I said, "Oh?" and reached for a spoon. Then I said, "What, Mama?"

"I don't feel so well."

"Is it flu?" I asked her.

"I think it's something more."

"I see," I said, and stirred the cocoa around and around, watching bubbles travel in circles. Then I said, "Well, the . . . yes, the doctor. We'll go to the doctor."

"I'm afraid to go to the doctor," my mother said.

I laid the spoon aside. I watched the bubbles continue to skate, slower and slower. Then I happened to glance over at my mother, who was sitting in her lawn chair hugging her stomach. It was true that she seemed unwell. Her face had

sharpened; her eyes had moved closer together somehow. I
didn't like the set of her shoulders. I said, "Mama?"

"Something is wrong with me, Charlotte," she said.

I had Julian drive us to the doctor. By suppertime she'd
been clapped in the hospital; by eight the next morning she'd
been operated on. I waited for word on a vinyl couch that
stuck to the backs of my legs. When Dr. Porter and the surgeon
walked toward me, I jumped up with a smacking sound. The
surgeon arrived first and developed a sudden interest in a still
life hanging behind me. "All we did," he said over his shoulder," "was close her up again." I didn't like his choice of
words. I stayed stubbornly silent, clutching my pocketbook.

"There was nothing else possible," Dr. Porter said. "I'm
sorry, Charlotte."

"That's all right," I said.

"It's c.a.," the surgeon told me.

"*Oh*, yes," I said. "Well, thank you very much."

"You can see her in a while," said Dr. Porter. "Are you
by yourself?"

"Saul is coming."

"Well. I'll be in touch."

I sank back onto the couch and watched them go. I
thought that walking in those thick-soled shoes would be like
wading through a sandbox. Then I noticed Saul plunging down
the corridor, his face remote and luminous. He passed me,
paused, raised a hand to his forehead and returned. "What's
c.a.?" I asked him.

"Cancer," he said, sitting down.

"Oh, I see. Of course."

He opened his Bible to the ribbon marker. Halfway down
the page, he suddenly stopped and looked over at me. We
stared at each other blankly, like two people at the windows of
separate trains.

After my mother returned from the hospital, her bedroom became the center of the house. She was too sick to get up again and she hated to be left alone. In that large, gloomy room, with its rotted silk draperies and bowlegged furniture, Jiggs memorized his spelling list, Miss Feather balanced the books, Linus made miniature swings and hung them from the branches of his bonsai trees. And my mother sat propped against a mountain of pillows, because lying flat was uncomfortable now. She even slept propped—or rather, spent the night propped, for I don't know when she really slept. Any time of night that I checked her she would just be sitting there, and the Texaco lights shining through the window lit the watchful hollows of her eyes. Bones that had been buried for the last fifty years were beginning to emerge in her face.

"When will I be up?" she asked at first.

"Soon, soon," we told her.

I felt that we were cowardly, but Saul said we should protect her as long as possible. We had some arguments about it. (This dying business was pointing up all our differences.) Then one day she asked me, "Please. When exactly will I start getting better?"

It was Sunday, a bright white Sunday in December, and Saul was not around. My only witness was Amos, stapling music sheets over in the armchair. I took a deep breath. I said, "Mama, I don't believe you'll ever be getting better."

My mother lost interest and turned away. She started smoothing the tufts on her quilt. "I hope you're remembering to mist my ferns," she said.

"Yes, Mama."

"I dreamed the tips were browning."

"They're not."

"Dr. Porter is a very fine person but I hated that surgeon man," she said. "Dr. . . . . Lewis? Loomis? I knew right away he wasn't worth much. Coming in ahead of time to get on my good side, cracking jokes, keeping his hands in his pockets— and plotting all along to rummage about in my innards. I think we ought to sue him, Charlotte."

"Mama, we can't do that."

"Certainly we can. I want my lawyer."

"You don't have a lawyer," I told her.

"Oh," she said. "Well. In that case."

She slumped a little. I thought the conversation had tired her. I stood up and said, "Why don't you try and sleep now, I'll go see about supper. Amos is here if you need something."

"I need to know the name of my problem," she said.

For a minute I didn't understand. Her problem? How would I know? I was still trying to figure out the name of *my* problem. But then she said, "My illness, Charlotte."

"It's cancer," I said.

She folded her hands on the quilt and grew still. I became aware of Amos; he had lowered his music sheets and was staring at me. His shucked-off moccasins lay gaping beneath his chair. I saw he had a hole in his sock that I would have to fix. Every thought seemed to come to me so clearly. "Don't wear that sock again until I've darned it," I said. I left.

Then there was a period when Mama didn't care to see me, barely answered when I spoke to her, sent the others out of the room for making too much noise and littering the floor with their torn envelopes and tangerine peels. She asked only for Saul. Wanted him to read to her from her big old family Bible: Psalms. She didn't like the rest of the Bible any more, people undertaking definite activities or journeying to specific towns. Saul would read until his voice cracked, and come downstairs pale and exhausted. "I did the best I could," he would say. You would think this was *his* mother. First he'd had Alberta and now he had Mama, and here I was with nobody.

"What more could I have done?" he asked.

"If you don't know, who does?" I said.

Her bedroom hung over our heads like some huge gray dirigible. She hulked in our minds; her absence filled the house.

I took to keeping the studio open at night. You'd be surprised at the people who decide to get photographed at ten or eleven p.m. if they pass by and see a place lit. They would stop at the bay window—solitary teenagers, men who couldn't sleep, housewives going out for tomorrow morning's milk. They would stare at my pictures, all my portraits of people bedecked with Alberta's clutter and dimmed by the crackling, imperfect light that seeped through my father's worn camera. Then they'd come inside and ask, "Are those your regular portraits?"

"What else?" I'd say.

"You mean I could have one like that too?"

"Of course."

And while I was loading the plates they'd drift around the studio, picking up an ermine muff, a celluloid fan, a three-cornered hat with gold braid . . .

Some people I photographed over and over, week after week—whenever they fell into a certain mood, it seemed. And this boy Bando, at the Texaco station: he would come by the first of every month, as soon as he got his paycheck. A hoodlum type, really, but in his pictures, with that light on his cheekbones and Grandpa Emory's fake brass sword at his hip, he took on a fine-edged, princely appearance that surprised me every time. *He* wasn't surprised, though. He would study his proofs the next day with a smile of recognition, as if he'd always known he could look this way. He would purchase every pose and leave, whistling.

Our sleep requirements changed. Our windows were lit till early morning, often. You would think the whole household had developed a fear of beds. Julian might be out with some girl, our only night-wanderer, but the rest of us found reasons to sit in the living room—reading, sewing, playing the piano, Linus carving bedposts from Tinker Toy sticks. Sometimes even the children got up, inventing urgent messages now that they had my attention. Selinda needed a costume; she'd forgotten to tell me. Jiggs had to ask, "Quick: what's five Q and five Q?"

"Is this important?"

"Oh, come on, Mom. Five Q and five Q."

"Ten Q."

"You're welcome."

"Ha ha," I said.

"Get it?"

"I *get* it, I get it," I said, and kissed the small nook that was the bridge of his nose.

Upstairs, my mother sat propped like some ancient, stately queen and listened to her own private psalmist.

But then she banished him. She shouted at Saul one suppertime so that all of us could hear, and a minute later he came down the stairs with his heavy, pausing tread and sank into his chair at the head of the table. "She wants *you*, Charlotte," he said.

"What happened?"

"She says she's tired."

"Tired of what?"

"Tired, just tired. I don't know," he said. "Pass the biscuits, Amos."

I went upstairs. Mama was sitting against the pillows with her mouth clamped, like a child in a huff. "Mama?" I said.

"I want my hair brushed, please."

I picked up her brush from the bureau.

"Those psalms, you wouldn't believe it," she said. "First so up and then so down, and then so up again."

"We'll find you something else," I said.

"I want Selinda to have my tortoise-shell necklace," said my mother. "It matches her eyes. I'm dying."

"All right," I said.

We greeted 1975 like an enemy. None of us had much hope for it. Saul lost several of his older members to the flu and had to be gone more than ever. The children were growing up without me. I spent all my time taking care of Mama. There was no position that felt right to her, nothing that sat easy on her stomach. She would get a craving for some food that was out of season or too expensive, and by the time I'd tracked it down she'd have lost her appetite and would only turn her face to the wall. "Take it away, take it away, don't bother me with that." Her pills didn't seem to work any more and she had to have hypodermics, which Dr. Sisk administered. She developed an oddly detailed style of worrying. "I hear a noise in the kitchen, Charlotte; I'm certain it's a burglar. He's helped himself to that leftover chicken you promised you would save for me." Or, "Why has Dr. Sisk not come? Go and check his room, please. He may have committed suicide. He's hung himself from an attic rafter by that gold chain belt in the cedar chest."

"Mama, I promise, everything's under control," I would tell her.

"That's easy for *you* to say."

It occurred to me that if I were the sullen spinster I had started out to be, this death would have meant the springing of my trap. Only it would have been useless even then; I'd have had a houseful of cats, no doubt, that I couldn't bear to leave. Newspapers piled to the ceiling. Money stuffed in the mattress.

"You're just waiting for me to die so that one of Saul's strays can have my room," she told me.

"Hush, Mama, drink your soup."

Then she asked me to sort her bureau drawers. "There may be some things I want burned," she said. I pulled out the drawers one by one and emptied them on her bed: withered elastic stockings, lemon verbena sachets, recipes torn from magazines and hairnets that clung to her fingers. She fumbled

through them. "No, no, take them back." What was she looking for, love letters? Diaries?

She felt in the bottom of her smallest desk drawer, came
up with something brown and stared at it a moment. Then,
"Here," she said. "Put this in the fire."

"What is it?"

"Burn it. If there isn't a fire, build one."

"All right," I said. I took it—some kind of photo in a
studio folder—and laid it beside me. "Do you want me to bring
the next drawer?"

"*Go,* Charlotte. Go burn it."

When she was angry, her face bunched in now as if gathered at the center by a drawstring. She was finally looking her
age: seventy-four, scooped out, caved in like a sunken pillow.
She raised one white, shaking forefinger. "*Fast!*" she said. Her
voice broke.

So I went. But as soon as I was out of the room I looked
at what she'd given me. Stamped across the front was "Ham-
mond Bros., Experienced Photographers"—surely no outfit in
Clarion. The folder was cheap, and hastily cut. The corners
didn't quite match.

Inside was a picture of my mother's true daughter.

I don't know how I knew that so immediately. Something
about the eyes, maybe—light-colored, triangular, expectant.
Or the dimples in her cheeks, or the merry, brimming smile.
The picture had been taken when she wasn't more than ten,
maybe younger. It was a soft-focus photo on unusually thin
paper: head only, and a ruffle at the neck, and a draggled bit of
ribbon holding back her pale, rather frowsy hair.

When had my mother found her? Why had she kept it a
secret?

I took the picture to my bedroom, locked the door, and
sat down in a wing chair to study it. The funny thing was that
in a vague way I felt connected to this little girl. I almost knew

her. We could have been friends. But I guessed from her unkempt hair and overdone ruffle that she came from a poor class of people. Migrant workers, maybe, or tenants in a trailer camp. No doubt she had grown up on wheels, stayed footloose and unreliable and remained on wheels, and had long ago left these parts. It should have been my life. It *was* my life, and she was living it while I was living hers, married to her true husband, caring for her true children, burdened by her true mother.

I slid the photo into my pocket. (I never considered destroying it.) And from then on I slid it into every pocket, and slept with it under my pillow at night. She was with me permanently. Often now as I moved around the house with bedpans and rubbing alcohol I was dreaming of her sleazy, joyful world. I imagined we would meet someday and trade stories of the ways we'd spent each other's life.

My mother began to ramble in her thoughts. I believe she just *allowed* herself to ramble, as a sort of holiday. Wouldn't anyone, in her position? When she had to, she could be as lucid as ever. But in her presence most people faltered, the children fell dumb, and even Saul found reasons to leave. It was just me and Mama—back to the old days. Mama sat nodding at the wall, I sewed emblems on Selinda's Girl Scout uniform. Little green stitches fastening down my mother's foggy memories. I thought about the household tasks—the mending, cooking, story-reading, temperature-taking, birthday cakes, dentist's and pediatrician's appointments—necessary for the rearing of a child. All those things my mother had managed, middle-aged though she had been, crippled with high blood pressure and varicose veins, so clumsy and self-conscious that the simplest trip for new school shoes was something to dread for days beforehand. I had never put it all together before. It seemed that the other girl's photo had released me in some way, let me step back to a reasonable distance and finally take an unhampered view of my mother.

"He had never even kissed a girl," she said. "I had to be the one to kiss him. He was so relieved."

"Really, Mama?"

"I suppose you think we made a lot of mistakes with you."

"Oh, no."

"We didn't give you a very happy childhood."

"Nonsense, Mama, I had a happy childhood."

In fact, maybe I did. Who knows?

"And his breath smelled of Juicy Fruit chewing gum. I have always considered Juicy Fruit a very trashy flavor."

"Me too," I said.

"My brother hardly ever comes to see me any more."

"He died, Mama. Remember?"

"Of course I remember. What do you take me for?"

"Aunt Aster sent you a card, though."

She tossed, as if throwing off some annoyance.

"If you like, I'll read it to you," I said.

She said, "How long am I going to be ruled by physical things? When do I get to be rid of this body?"

"I don't know, Mama."

"Bring me my cigarettes," she said.

(She didn't smoke.)

I laid aside my sewing and slipped out of the room. Sometimes I just had to. I went swiftly down the stairs, keeping my mind very blank and cold. But in the living room I found rumpled magazines, cast-off shoes, Linus's doll chairs needling the floor, Amos sprawled on the couch with a newspaper. I stopped and pressed a hand to my forehead. Amos looked up. He said, "Shall I go sit with her a while?"

"No, that's all right," I said.

"Aren't you tired?"

"No."

He studied me. "I never really knew you before," he said finally.

I had a feeling that he didn't know me now, either.

For I was numb, and observed my life as calmly as a woman made of ice, but Amos thought I was strong and brave. He told me so. A thousand times—peering into Mama's darkened room, bringing me coffee, sending me out for a walk in a world that was, surprisingly, going through summer—he would pause and say, "I don't know how you manage this."

"There isn't any managing to be done," I told him.

"I used to think you were only beautiful," he said now.

"Only what?"

"I didn't understand you. Now I see everyone grabbing for pieces of you, and still you're never diminished. Clutching on your skirts and they don't even slow you down. And you're the one who told her the truth; I heard you. Said the word out loud. Cancer. You sail through this house like a moon, you're strong enough for all of them."

I should have argued. (I should have laughed.) But all I said was, "No . . ." and paused. Then Amos laid aside his paper, and unfolded himself from the couch and took hold of my shoulders and kissed me. He was so slow and deliberate, I could have stopped him any time; but I didn't. His mouth was softer than Saul's. His hands were warmer. He lacked Saul's gaunt, driven intenseness, and made me see that everything was simpler than I'd realized.

My life grew to be all dreams; there was no reality whatsoever. Mama fell into stupors and could not be roused. The children looked like faded little sketches of themselves. My customers drifted in and out again, oddly attired in feather boas, top hats, military medals. Saul didn't talk any more and often when I woke in the night I'd find him sitting on the edge of the bed, unnaturally still, watching me.

Amos met me in vacant rooms, in the steamy attic, in the bend of an unused stairway. We could be discovered at any time and so we held back, for now; but without even moving he could reel me in to him. It was the end of summer and his skin had a polished, brassy glow. His face had grown sleek and well-fed looking. When he lifted me up in his arms I felt I had left all my troubles on the floor beneath me like gigantic concrete shoes.

I loved him for not being Saul, I suppose. Or for being a younger, happier Saul. He carried no freight of past wrongs and debts; that was why I loved him.

"When this is over with your mother, I'll take you away," he said. "I understand that you can't leave now."

Actually, he didn't understand. I would have left. I wanted to get out, throw all the old complexities off, make a clean start. But I was trying to stay faithful to his picture of me and so I only nodded.

"We'll go walking down the street together in a town we've never been to," he said. "People will ask me, 'Where'd you *get* her? How'd you find her?' 'She's been sleeping,' I'll tell them. 'She's been waiting. My brother was keeping her for me.'"

We looked at each other. We were not cruel people, either one of us. We weren't unkind. So why did we take such joy in this? My wickedness made me feel buoyant, winged. Gliding past a mirror, I was accompanied by someone beautiful: her hair filled with lights, eyes deep with plots, gypsyish dress a splash of color in the dusk. When Amos and I met in public, our hands touched, clung, slid off each other and parted, while we ourselves went our separate ways blank-faced and gloating like thieves.

I photographed Miss Feather swathed in a black velvet opera cape, holding a silver pistol that was actually a table lighter. "This will be for my great-niece LaRue, who never comes to visit," she said. "Make up several prints, if you will."

"All right," I said.

"For my other great-nieces, too. Who also never come to visit."

"I'll have them by tomorrow," I said.

It was night. I was tired. Mama had dropped off and I was trying to catch up on my work. But I could hardly see to focus the camera; everything was haloed. "I believe I'll go to bed," I told Miss Feather.

"No, wait, please."

"I need some sleep."

"But what about Saul? I mean to say," said Miss Feather, "Saul is not himself these days."

"Who *is?*"

She fumbled at her throat, cast off her cape, and rushed at me. A tiny, excitable woman waving a silver pistol. "Now listen, please," she told me. "I had this in mind to say for some time: he's your husband. Would you like to take a little vacation together? I could stay with the children."

"*Vacation,* Miss Feather. I consider it a vacation if I can make it out of Mama's bedroom."

"But . . . dear heart—"

"Thank you anyway," I told her.

I went upstairs, took off my shoes, and sagged on the edge of the bed. Saul wasn't there. He had taken to going on long walks in the dark. I was on my own, and felt free to slip a hand in my skirt pocket and pull out my true self's photograph. She smiled back at me, carefree and reckless, but my eyes were too tired to make any sense of her. It seemed she had arrived unassembled. I couldn't put her together.

How did you turn out, finally? What kind of grownup are you now?

Late in December they took Mama away and put her in the hospital. I had hoped to avoid that but Dr. Porter said I was getting strange-looking. Besides, he said, she might not even notice. She was hardly ever conscious any more. They hooked her up to a number of cords and dials. She lay silent, with her eyes tight shut. I imagined she was doing it deliberately—not sleeping or comatose but closing me out, hugging her secret clawed monster. I felt jealous. The nurses told me to go on home but I stayed, stubbornly gripping the arms of my chair.

Amos brought me a Big Mac—the smell of beautiful, everyday life. When I wouldn't come away with him he laid it on the table beside me and loped off down the corridor. His moccasins made a gentle scolding sound. Then Julian danced in all edgy and skittish, dressed up as if for a night at the races. He gave me a note from Linus: *I can't visit hospitals. Can't manage. Taking the Children to pizza palace, is my sympathy gift to You.* I thanked Julian and he danced out again.

Saul stooped in the doorway, took stock of the room and then entered. He settled in the armchair next to mine, tugging at his bony black cloth knees. His head lunged forward awkwardly. "Have you eaten?" he whispered.

"Yes," I said.

The Big Mac sat untouched on the table; the smell of it had made me full.

"How is she?"

"The same. You don't have to whisper."

He cleared his throat. He set his Bible on his lap, took out his reading glasses and polished them with the end of his tie. Then he put them on and opened the Bible. I went back to studying Mama. She reminded me of a withered balloon. All those cords were just to hold her down; without them she'd lift up, level and sedate, and go wafting out the window. I snickered. I glanced over at Saul, hoping he hadn't noticed. He was looking not at the Bible but straight ahead of him. His face was grim.

"Saul?" I said.

His eyes came to rest on me.

"Are you all right?"

"I'm eternally visiting deathbeds," he said. "Even more than other preachers."

"You do seem to go to a lot," I said.

"Maybe it's because I'm so poor at them."

"You are?"

"I don't know what to say at them. And I don't like dying people."

"Never mind," I told him.

"Sometimes," he said, "I believe we're given the same lessons to learn, over and over, exactly the same experiences, till we get them right. Things keep circling past us."

I thought of a merry-go-round, little dappled horses. To me, it seemed soothing. But Saul clamped his Bible shut and leaned toward me, looking into my eyes. "Till we get it straight," he said. "Forgive, or settle up, or make the proper choice. Whatever we failed to do the first time."

"Well, maybe so," I said.

"I keep telling myself that."

"I see."

He made me uneasy, a little. Maybe he sensed it, because he relaxed suddenly and sat back in his chair. "Well," he said, "that's what I wanted to say to you."

"I see," I said again.

"Will you come home with me, Charlotte?"

"I can't."

"You know she won't wake up. You heard what Dr. Porter said."

"Saul, I just can't," I said. "You go."

And he did, after a minute. The rustle he made while getting himself together was an irritation. I waited, keeping my face turned aside, wondering why he paused so long at the door. But finally he was gone.

Then I had my mother to myself. For I couldn't let loose of her yet. She was like some unsolvable math problem you keep straining at, worrying the edges of, chafing and cursing.

She had used me up, worn me out, and now was dying without answering any really important questions or telling me a single truth that mattered. A mound on the bed, opaque, intact. I was furious.

Around midnight, she said, "There is too great a weight on my feet."

I bent forward to look at her. In the bluish glow of the nightlight I could make out her small, dazed eyes. I said, "Mama?"

"What is this on my feet?" she asked. Her voice was parched and broken. "And my arms, they're all strung up to something. What's happened?"

"You're in the hospital," I told her.

"Take that blanket or whatever off my feet, please, Charlotte."

"Mama, are you all the way awake?"

"My *feet*."

I stood up and searched my skirt pockets, my blouse pocket, and nearly panicked, till I remembered my cardigan. "Mama," I said, "look." I turned on the reading lamp at the head of her bed. She flinched and closed her eyes. I held the photograph in front of her face. "Look, Mama."

"But the light."

"It's important," I told her. "Who is this a picture of?"

She rolled her head back and forth, protesting, but opened her eyes a slit. Then closed them. "Oh, me," she said.

"Who is it, Mama?"

"Me, I said. Me as a child."

I took the picture away and stared at it. "Are you sure?" I asked.

She nodded, uninterested.

"But . . . I thought it would be your true daughter. The one they mixed up in the hospital."

"Hospital?" she said. She opened her eyes again and let

them travel in a slow, frowning arc across the shadowy ceiling. "I never gave my permission to be brought to any hospital."

"The one you had a baby in, Mama. Remember you had a baby?"

"A surprise," my mother said.

"That's right."

"Like a present. A doll in a box."

"Well..."

"I can't imagine how it happened, we hardly ever did much."

"Never mind *that,* Mama; the baby. You didn't think it was yours."

"It?" she said. She seemed to pull herself together. "It wasn't an it, it was you, Charlotte. The baby was you."

"But you said they mixed me up in the hospital."

"Why would I say that? Oh, this is all so ... it's much too bright in here."

I turned the light off. "Let me get this straight," I said. "You never thought that I was someone else's. The notion never occurred to you."

"No, no. Maybe you misunderstood," she said. "Maybe ... I don't know ..." She closed her eyes. "Please lighten my feet."

I couldn't think what to ask next. I had lost my bearings. Oh, it wasn't that I doubted my memory; I was still sure of that. (Or almost sure.) But the picture! For now I saw that of course it was Mama. Obviously it was. And here I'd found so much in that little girl's eyes, imagined such a connection between us!

"My feet, Charlotte."

I slipped the picture back in my pocket, then, and went to the foot of her bed and lifted off the folded spread. I hung it over a chair. I returned to her, avoiding tubes and cords, careful not to jar her, and more gently than I'd ever done anything in my life, I laid my cheek against my mother's.

She died a few days later, and was buried from Holy Basis Church with Saul officiating. Her coffin seemed oddly narrow. Maybe I'd made up her fatness, too.

The funeral was well attended because she was the preacher's mother-in-law. None of the congregation thought much of me (I wouldn't come to Sewing Circle, lacked the proper attitude, really was not worthy of Saul in any way), but they were very kind and said what they were supposed to. I answered in a voice that seemed to come from beside my right ear. This death had taken me by surprise; I'd lost someone more important than I'd expected to lose.

After the funeral, I went through a period of time when I was unusually careful of people. Everything they offered me, I tried to accept: Miss Feather's tea, cup after cup; Dr. Sisk's little winter bouquets; even Saul's prayers, which he said in silence so I wouldn't take offense but I knew, I felt them circling me. Sometimes when I was sitting up with Jiggs (for a while there, he had nightmares), Saul would wake and come search me out, and stand in the doorway in his shabby pajamas. "Are you all right?" he'd ask.

"I'm fine."

"I thought something might be wrong."

"Oh, no."

"I woke and you weren't there."

"Are *you* all right?" I said.

"Yes, certainly."

"Don't catch cold."

Then he'd wait for a minute, and run his fingers through his hair and finally turn and stagger back to bed.

I saw that all of us lived in a sort of web, criss-crossed by strings of love and need and worry. Linus cocked his head and searched our faces; Amos sent his music calling through the house. Selinda was floating free now in her early teens, but still kept touching down to make sure of us at unexpected moments. And Julian had a way of leaving his hand on people's shoulders like something forgotten, meanwhile whistling and looking elsewhere.

"I won't hurry you," Amos said.

I looked at him.

"I know what you're going through," he told me.

For we never met in vacant rooms any more—or if he found me in one by accident and put his arms around me I only felt fond and distracted. I was saddened by his chambray shirt, with the elbow patches that I had sewn on in some long ago, light-hearted time. It appeared that we were all taking care of each other, in ways an outsider might not notice.

So I survived. Baked their cakes. Washed their clothes. Fed their dog. Stepped through my studio doorway one evening and fell into the smell of work, a deep, rich, comforting smell: chemicals and high-gloss paper and the gritty, ancient metal of my father's camera. I turned on the lights and took the CLOSED sign from the door. Not ten minutes later, along came Bando from the filling station. He said he wanted a picture like Miss Feather's: cape and silver pistol. Could I do it? Would the cape fit, was the pistol real?

"Certainly it's real," I told him. "You see it, you feel it: it's real."

"No, what I mean is . . ."

"Sit beside the lamp, please."

As soon as he was gone I developed his pictures; I was so glad to be busy again. I came from the darkroom with a sheaf of wet prints and found Amos in the doorway. He was leaning there watching me. I said, "Amos!"

"You're back at work," he said.

"Yes, well, only Bando."

I hung the prints. Bando's face gazed down at me, clean and still, like something locked in amber. "Isn't it funny?" I said. "In ordinary life he's not nearly so fine. But my father would never approve of these; they're not really real, he would say."

"What's your father got to do with it?" Amos asked.

"Well ..."

"This studio's been yours for, what? Sixteen, seventeen years now. It's been yours nearly as long as it was his."

"Well," I said. "Yes, but ..." I turned and looked at him. "That's true, it has," I said.

"And still you act surprised when somebody wants you to take his picture. You have to decide if you'll do it, every time. A seventeen-year temporary position! Lord God."

It dawned on me finally that he was angry. But I didn't know what for. I wiped my hands on my skirt and went over to him. "Amos?" I said.

He stepped back. He had suddenly grown very still.

"You're not coming away with me, are you, Charlotte," he said.

"Coming—?"

I realized that I wasn't.

"You're much too content the way you are. Snow White and the four dwarfs."

"No, it's ... what? No, it's just that lately, Amos, it's seemed to me I'm so tangled with other people here. More connected than I'd thought. Don't you see that? How can I ever begin to get loose?"

"I'd assumed it was your mother," he said. "I assumed it was *duty*, that you'd leave in an instant if not for her. Turns out I was wrong. Here you are, free to go, but then you always were, weren't you? You could have left any day of your life, but hung around waiting to be sprung. Passive. You're passive, Charlotte. You stay where you're put. Did you ever really intend to leave?"

I didn't think my voice would work, but it did. "Why, of course," I said.

"Then I pity you," he said, but I could tell he didn't feel a bit of pity. He looked at me from a height, without bending his head. His hands in his pockets were fists. "It's not only me you've fooled, it's yourself," he said. "I can get out, but you've let yourself get buried here and even helped fill in the grave. Every year you've settled for less, tolerated more. You're the kind who thinks tolerance is a virtue. You're proud of letting anyone be anything they choose; it's *their* business, you say, never mind whose toes they step on, even your own . . ."

He stopped, maybe because of the look on my face. Or maybe he had just run down. He took one fist from his pocket and rubbed his mouth with the back of his hand.

"Well, thanks for the example," he said finally. "I'm leaving, before the same thing happens to me."

"Amos?"

But he was gone, not a pause or a backward glance. I heard the front door slam. I didn't know what to do next. I stood looking all around me in a stunned, hopeless way—at my dusty equipment, stacks of props, Alberta's furniture, which had never (I saw now) been sorted and discarded as Saul had promised but simply sifted in with our own. At the crumbling buildings across the street: the Thrift Shop, newsstand, liquor store, Pei Wing the tailor . . . not a single home in the lot, come to think of it. Everyone else had moved on, and left us stranded here between the Amoco and the Texaco.

I stood there so long I must have been in a kind of trance. I watched a soft snowstorm begin, proceeding so slowly and so vertically that it was hard to tell, at first, whether the snow was falling or the house was rising, floating imperceptibly into the starless blue night.

After Amos went away, I became very energetic. I had things to do; I was preparing to get out.

First I discarded clothing, books, knick-knacks, pictures. I lugged pieces of furniture across the street to the Thrift Shop. I gave my mother's lawn chair to Pei Wing, the plants to Saul's choir leader, the Sunday china to Holy Basis Church. I threw away rugs and curtains and doilies. I packed the doll things in cartons and put them in the attic. What I was aiming for was a house with the bare, polished look of a bleached skull. But I don't know, it was harder than I'd thought. Linus kept making *new* doll things. I packed those away, too. The piano grew new layers of magazines and keys. I had the Salvation Army come and cart the piano off. Objects spilled out of the children's bedrooms and down the stairs. I sent the objects back. Strangely enough, no one asked where all the furniture had gone.

The parlor became a light-filled, wallpapered cavern, containing a couch, two chairs, and a lamp, with blanched squares where the pictures used to hang. But still I wasn't satisfied. I skulked around the echoing rooms, newly drab in a narrow gray skirt I had saved from the trashcan, discontentedly watching Jiggs skate the bare floors in his stocking feet.

Then I discarded people. I stopped answering the phone, no longer nodded to acquaintances, could not be waylaid in the grocery store. Skimming down the sidewalk, noticing someone I knew heading toward me, I felt my heart sink. I would cross the street immediately. I didn't want to be bothered. They were using up such chunks of my life, with their questions, comments, gossip, inquiries after my health. They were siphoning me off into teachers' conferences and charity drives. Before Selinda's school play they made me waste twenty minutes, fiddling with my coat buttons and wondering when the curtain would go up. What did I have to do with Selinda, anyway? At this rate I would never get out.

I had some difficulty discarding what was in the studio and so I closed it off. I shut both doors and locked them. Sometimes when I was sitting in the living room I heard people knock on the outside door and call for me. "Lady? Picture lady? What's the matter, aren't you working no more? I been counting on this!" I listened, with my hands folded in my lap. I was surprised by how many people counted on my pictures. I was surprised by a lot of things. The flurry of my life had died down, the water had cleared so that finally I could see what was there.

But no one else could. My family pestered me, hounded me. They thought I had something left to give them. Well, I *tried* to tell them. I said, "You'll have to manage on your own from now on." They just looked baffled. Asked me to cut their hair, sew buttons on their shirts. Saul kept trying to start these pointless conversations. Really, he'd only married me because he saw me sticking with my mother. He saw I wouldn't have the gumption to leave a place. Him and his I-know-you-love-me's, I-know-you-won't-leave-me's; I should have realized. "This marriage isn't going well," I told him.

But he said, "Charlotte, everything has its bad patches."

"I need to take a wilderness course."

"Wilderness?"

"Learn to live on my own with no equipment. Cover great distances. In the desert and the Alps and such."

"But we don't have any deserts here."

"I know."

"And we don't have any Alps."

"I know."

"We don't even have snow all that often."

"Saul," I said, "don't you understand? I have never, ever been anywhere. I live in the house I was born in. I live in the house my *mother* was born in. My children go to the same school I did and one even has the same teacher. When I had that teacher she was just starting out and scared to death and pretty as a picture; now she's a dried-up old maid and sends Selinda home for not wearing a bra."

"Certainly," said Saul. "Things keep coming around,

didn't I tell you? You and *I* keep coming around, Charlotte, year by year, changed in little ways; we'll work things through eventually."

"It's not worth it, though," I said.

"Not worth it?"

"It takes too great a toll."

He folded both my hands in his, with his face very calm and preacherly. Probably he didn't know how hard he was gripping. "Wait a while," he said. "This will pass. We all have . . . just wait a while. Wait."

I waited. What was I waiting for? It seemed I hadn't yet discarded all I should have. There were still some things remaining.

Jiggs reminded me of the P.T.A. meeting; he saw it on the UNICEF calendar. He was seven now and industrious, organizational, a natural-born chairman. "Eight o'clock, and wear your red dress," he told me.

"I don't have that dress any more and I don't want to go to any meetings."

"It's fun, they serve cookies. Our class is making the Kool-Aid."

"I have spent my life at the Clarion P.T.A. What's the purpose?"

"I don't know, but I'm sure there is one," said Jiggs. He peered at the calendar again. "The thirteenth is Muhammad's birthday. The fifth was World Day of Prayer. Mother, did you enjoy World Day of Prayer?"

"I'm sorry, honey, I didn't know they were having it."

"You should have looked ahead of time."

"My idea of a perfect day," I told him, "is an empty square on the calendar. That's all I ask."

"Well, then," said Jiggs. He adjusted his glasses and ran his finger across the page. "In the month of March, you'll have three perfect days."

"Three? Only three?"

I looked down at the back of his neck—concave, satiny. Very slowly, I began to let myself imagine his mother. She would ride into town on a Trailways bus, wearing something glorious and trashy spun of Lurex. I would meet her when she arrived. I would bring Jiggs with me. I would at long last give him up.

That morning Linus and Miss Feather were helping at the church bazaar; I had the place to myself. I sent the children to school and gave the house a final cleaning, dispensing with all the objects that had sprouted in the night—rolled socks, crumpled homework papers, and a doll's toy dollhouse no bigger than a sugar cube, filled with specks of furniture. (I didn't check to see what *kind* of furniture; I feared to find another dollhouse tucked inside that one.)

Then I took a bath and dressed in a fresh skirt and blouse. The mirror showed me someone stark and high-cheekboned, familiar in an unexpected way. My eyes had a sooty look and you would think from the spots of color on my cheeks that I was feverish. I wasn't, though. I felt very cold and heavy.

The dog seemed to know that I was going and kept following me too closely, moaning and nudging the backs of my knees with his nose. He got on my nerves. I unlocked my studio door and pushed him inside. "Goodbye, Ernest," I said. Then I straightened and saw the greenish light that filtered through the windows—a kind of light they don't have anyplace else. Oh, I've never had the knack of knowing I was happy right while the happiness was going on. I closed the door and passed back through the house, touching the worn, smudged woodwork, listening to absent voices, inhaling the smell of school paste and hymnals. It didn't look as if I'd be able to go through with this after all.

But once you start an action, it tends to bear you along.

All I could hope for was to be snagged somewhere. In the sunporch, maybe, circling the phone, waiting for news that Jiggs had a sniffle and was being sent home early. In the kitchen, taking forever to make a cup of instant coffee. Absently pouring a bowl of cereal. Something besides cereal fell from the box—a white paper packet. I plucked it out and opened it. Inside was a stamped tin badge, on which a cartoon man walked swiftly toward me with his feet the biggest part of him. And along the bottom, my own personal message.

Keep on truckin'.

15

We drove slowly, looking for a bank that stayed open Friday nights. We left Perth behind, entered the next town and then the next. These places were strung together like beads, no empty spots between them but ravelings of Tastee-Freezes, seashell emporiums, and drive-in movies. It was dark enough now so I could see the actors' faces on the screens. But all I saw of Jake and Mindy was the gold line edging each of their profiles, sometimes lit other colors by the neon signs we passed. Mindy was craning forward, searching the buildings, biting her lower lip. Jake was sunk low in his seat like someone sick or beaten, and he hardly bothered to look out the window.

"Maybe in this state, banks don't have Friday hours," Mindy said.

Jake didn't answer.

"Jake?"

He stirred. "Sure they do," he said.

"How do you know? What if we end up driving all night, Jake, ride right off the bottom of Florida. Shouldn't we stop and get a store to cash this thing?"

"Well, stores, now, they might tend to make more of a to-do," Jake said. "Be more apt to remember us later."

"But I'm tired! I got a crick in my neck."

Jake let his head turn, following a likely-looking office building.

"If I don't eat by six I faint," said Mindy. "And look, it's almost seven."

"Well, there now, Mindy," Jake said absently.

"You know I got low blood sugar."

"Really? You want some sugar?"

"*No* I don't want sugar."

"No trouble at all, Mindy, I got it right here." He searched his jacket, accidentally poking me with one elbow. "Look at here. Domino sugar."

The packets were worn and grimy by now. He held them out, a double handful. "Never say I don't come prepared."

"Jake Simms," said Mindy, "don't you know anything? It's not sugar I need, that would be stupid."

He lowered his hands. He looked over at me. "Can you figure that?" he asked.

"Well . . ."

"She's got low blood sugar, but she don't want to *eat* sugar."

"She must know, I guess."

He shook his head, looking down at the packets. "I just don't see this, Mindy," he said. "You don't even make sense. How come you run after me so hard if it turns out there's no way I can please you?"

"*Me* run after *you?*" said Mindy. "Oh, go ahead, gripe and groan. Blame it all on me. Then ask yourself what you told me last Fourth of July. Go on, ask yourself."

He gave me a quick glance, sideways, from under his blunt lashes.

"What'd you tell her?" I asked.

He set his mouth, crammed the sugar back into his pockets.

"Told me he never had come to rest with anyone but me," said Mindy. "Said he didn't know why, it was just the way he felt. We were eating a picnic lunch, he had done right poorly in a demolition derby. I told him that derby didn't matter a bit. 'To *my* mind,' I told him, 'you will always be like the first time I saw you driving: real swift and fine, in your white western jacket that got tore up later in that derby over by Washington.' And that's when he said what he said. Asked if I would marry him."

"I never did," said Jake.

"Well, you said you could see that it might someday come to pass."

"You just got it all twisted around to suit your purposes."

"No, Jake," she said. "Believe me, I do not. It's *you* that twists. Can't you see what spits you in the face? For every time you run from me, there's another time you run *after* me, deliver yourself up to me. You say, 'Mindy, I'm yours. You're all I got.' You call out under my window, you drive by my house in the night and I see your headlights slide across my ceiling. You get me on the telephone: 'Everybody's mad at me and the world don't look so hot. Can't you come on out and keep me company?' "

"You just like to exaggerate," said Jake.

"What you said was, 'I can see that we might someday find ourselves married.' "

"If I did, I don't recall it."

" 'Like, if you was to end up pregnant or something,' you said."

There was a silence.

"You said, 'What do I want to keep buffeting back and forth for, anyhow? Why don't I just give up?'"

In the sudden glow of a movie marquee Jake's face appeared sallow, unhealthy. The skin beneath his eyes was a bruised color.

"Isn't that the truth?" Mindy asked him.

"Hold it, I found us a bank. Pull over."

She slammed on the brakes, throwing both of us forward, and veered into a parking space. Jake held himself upright with a hand on the dashboard. "There was something I was meaning to ask," he said slowly. "All this crazy talk has put it right out of my head."

We waited.

Then his face cleared. "How much money you got?" he said to Mindy.

"Is that all you can think about?"

"I mention it in case you want a hot dog or something, while me and Charlotte are in the bank."

"Oh," she said. "Well, I got enough."

"See that little diner joint? Meet you there in five minutes. Maybe ten."

"You want me to order *you* two something?"

"Naw," said Jake.

"Aren't you hungry?"

"Oh, why, well sure," he said, "but that hot dog is just to hold you, Mindy. After we get our money we're going somewheres good. Isn't that right, Charlotte. Charlotte?"

"A steak place would be nice," said Mindy.

"Steak place, any place, I don't care," he told her. "Scoot."

Mindy opened the door and slid out. We followed. Jake touched a finger to Mindy's wrist. "Bye," he said.

"Bye," she said, and left, swinging her heart-shaped purse.

It was a warm, buggy night that smelled of caramel. The

streets were nearly deserted. To our right was a beige brick cube with aluminum letters across the front: SECOND FEDERAL. We climbed the steps and spun through the revolving door. My face felt tight in the sudden coolness. Tubes of harsh white light made us blink, and our feet were hushed by fuzzy carpeting. I took my place behind a man in a business suit.

"Why this *here* line?" Jake asked me. "This is the longest."

Of course it was longest. I was going to be leaving soon and I didn't want events to move too quickly. As if he guessed that, Jake moved in closer behind me. "Charlotte," he said in my ear.

"Hmm?"

"I don't want you pulling nothing funny. Understand?"

I nearly laughed. I wondered what he imagined I could do. Leap the teller's grate in a single bound? Sign my check in some suspicious way? *Charlotte Emory, hostage.* The teller wouldn't even raise her eyebrows. She would glance at my signature indifferently, as if I'd stated some natural condition or occupation. Oh, I knew better by now than to count on other people for help. "Don't be silly," I said to Jake. He must have seen that I meant it; he dropped back. His nylon jacket rustled. The man in the business suit left, folding a sheaf of bills.

"I'd like to cash a traveler's check," I said to the teller. She looked bored. I signed my name with a chained ball-point pen and passed the check through the grate. In return she counted out a hundred dollars in twenties. I counted once more and then gave my place up to a red-headed lady who was dabbing her nose with a Kleenex.

Out on the street, Jake said, "Well, that wasn't so hard."

"No," I said.

"Nothing to it."

"No."

We passed a shoestore, darkened now, and then a florist's

where ugly tropical flowers glowed behind glass. We reached the diner—a railroad car surrounded by a picket fence. Through one long, greasy window we saw Mindy with her back to us, her elbows on the counter, twisting idly on her stool so her skirt belled out and swirled. We stood watching as if we had nowhere else to go, no plans in mind at all. Jake gave a sudden, sharp sigh.

"I was fixing to leave her," he said.

I nodded.

"But I can't," he said. "She's right, you know. I have some ties to her."

Mindy hoisted a hot dog into the air; she was wiping her face in the crook of her elbow, which from here seemed as delicate as a vine or tendril.

"I'm going to end up married to her, ain't I, Charlotte."

"Well, I guess that maybe you are, Jake," I said.

"I've done myself in. Ain't I? Just going to end up trucking along in that life she wants."

I looked at him.

"Gold and avocado," said Jake. "Patricia curtains. Babies. See what I've come to? What you staring at?"

"Nothing," I said. "Here."

"What's this?"

It was money, as he could plainly see. Five new twenty-dollar bills. I had to fold his fingers around them. He said, "Charlotte?"

"I'm leaving now," I told him.

His mouth fell open.

"I can't stay on forever, Jake. You knew I'd have to go sometime."

"No, wait," he said. His voice had turned harsh and raspy.

"Tell Mindy goodbye for me."

"Charlotte, but . . . see, I can't quite manage without you just yet. Understand? I've got this pregnant woman on my hands, got all these . . . Charlotte, it ain't so bad if you're *with* us, you see. You act like you take it all in stride, like this is the way life really does tend to turn out. You mostly wear this little smile. I mean, we know each other, Charlotte. Don't we?"

"Yes," I said.

"And anyhow!" he said. He suddenly lifted his chin. He thrust the money in his pocket and stood straighter, teetering slightly from heel to toe. "I don't know why I'm *begging,* you can't leave anyhow. I've got your money."

"You can have it," I told him.

"Then how would you travel? Just tell me that."

"Oh well, I'll . . . go to Travelers' Aid," I said.

"And your medal!"

"What?"

"I guess you want it back, don't you."

"Medal? Oh, the——"

"Well, you won't get it. I aim to keep it."

"That's all right," I said.

I held out my hand. I didn't want to just walk away without shaking hands. But Jake wouldn't take it. His chin was still tilted and he watched me from across the two polished planes of his cheekbones. In the end I had to give up.

"Well, goodbye," I told him.

And I turned and set off in the direction we'd come from, where it seemed most likely I'd find a bus terminal.

Then Jake said, "Charlotte?"

I stopped.

"Keep going and I'll shoot you, Charlotte."

I started walking again.

"I'm aiming now. Hear? I've took the safety off. It's loaded. It's pointed at your heart."

My footsteps had a steady sound, like rain.

"Charlotte!"

I continued up the street, already feeling the hole that

would open in my back. I passed an elderly couple in evening clothes. Still no shot rang out. I saw now that it never would. I released my breath, marveling at my slipperiness: I had glided through so many dangers and emerged unscathed. As smooth as silk I swerved around a child, passed a glass-boxed woman in front of a theater. I reached the end of the block and looked back. There he stood, surprisingly small, still watching me. His collar was raised, his shoulders were hunched. His hands were thrust deep in his pockets. Come to think of it, I wasn't so unscathed after all.

16

The police never did recapture Jake Simms. As far as I know, they've given up the search. I told them he was going to Texas, anyway.

There is somebody new in Mama's old room: a drunk from the mourners' bench who used to be an opera singer. His name is Mr. Bentham. On good days his voice is beautiful. And Miss Feather is with us the same as always, though Dr. Sisk has moved away. He married a woman from the church last July and lives in a ranch house on the other side of town.

Julian still works at the radio shop, in between his lapses; Selinda still floats in and out of our lives, and no one has yet come for Jiggs. But Linus has stopped building dollhouse furniture and moved on to the dolls themselves: diminutive wooden people, fully jointed. Their joints are little fragments of straight pins. Their faces are drawn with a needle dipped in ink. They have distinctive features, coloring, and clothes, but share an expression of surprise, as if wondering how they got here.

And I still wheel my camera around, recording upsidedown people in unexpected costumes. But I've come to believe that their borrowed medals may tell more truths than they hide. While Saul grips his pulpit as firmly as always, and studies his congregation. No doubt they are suspended in a lens of his own, equally truthful, equally flawed.

Sometimes, when Saul can't sleep, he turns his head on the pillow and asks if I'm awake. We may have had a hard time that day: disagreed, misunderstood, come to one more invisible parting or tiny, jarring rearrangement of ourselves. He lies on his back in the old sleigh bed and starts to wonder: will everything work out? Is he all right, am I all right, are we happy, at least in some limited way? Maybe we ought to take a trip, he says. Didn't I use to want to?

But I tell him no. I don't see the need, I say. We have been traveling for years, traveled all our lives, we are traveling still. We couldn't stay in one place if we tried. Go to sleep, I say.

And he does.